**Also by Mark Binder**

*The Brothers Schlemiel*

*The Bedtime Story Book*

*Classic Stories for Boys and Girls*

*The World's Best Challah*

*Tall Tales, Whoppers and Lies*

*Dead at Knotty Oak*

*Crumbs Don't Count*
*(The Rationalization Diet)*

# a hanukkah present

## Mark Binder

Light Publications

Cover photo by Kristine Slipson
Edited by Patty Tanalksi
Design by Beth Hellman
Design consultation by Real Advertising
Marketing consultation by John Horton
Thanks to all my readers and listeners, especially Jim Rosenberg, Christina Fischer, Vida Hellman, Rachel,Max, and Elaine K. Binder. Thanks to the Rhode Island Bureau of Jewish Education.

Stories in this collection have appeared in: *Cricket Magazine, The Jewish Daily Forward, Washington Jewish Week, The Shofar, Being Jewish, The Observer, American Jewish World, The Jewish Chronicle, Jewish Western Bulletin, The Jewish Journal, Arizona Jewish Post, Greater Phoenix Jewish News, Chicago JUF News, Chicago Jewish Star, Charlotte Jewish News, American Jewish World, Jewish Free Press, The Chelmsford Independent, The Jewish Advocate & Jewish Times, Ohio Jewish Chronicle, The Wisconsin Jewish Chronicle, The School Magazine...*

ISBN 978-0-9702642-6-8
Library of Congress Control Number: 2007906087

Printed in the United States of America
10 9 8 7 6 5 4 3 2 1

Light Publications
PO Box 2462
Providence, RI 02906
U. S. A.
www.lightpublications.com

# Contents

Welcome

Glossary

# Welcome

Warm lights burning, the smell of delicious food, and the gathering of family. Do you hear the sound of laughter from the midwinter party?

The name of the village is Chelm—you pronounce it like you've got something stuck in your throat. If it was written "Helm," it wouldn't feel the same. For the same reason, throughout this book, the name of the holiday is spelled, "Chanukah."

In popular tradition, Chelm is considered a village of fools, but if we listen closely we may discover they have their moments of brilliance.

For instance, gifts, as Shmeenie Schlemiel says, are wonderful things, but they aren't essential. The essential ingredients are friends and the stories we tell each other on those cold winter nights.

# The Lethal Latkes

The villagers of Chelm dreaded Chanukah. It wasn't the holiday itself. They loved lighting the candles, spinning the dreidel, and retelling the stories of the Maccabees and the miracle of the lights. All in all, Chanukah was a wonderful festival, except for one thing—Mrs. Chaipul's latkes, which were served in great abundance at the annual Chanukah party.

Mrs. Chaipul's latkes were not good. They were really not good. It wasn't that they were too greasy (which they were), or that they were burned (which they sometimes were), or even that they were too heavy (which they always were), it was the smell. There was something slightly sickening about the smell of Mrs. Chaipul's potato pancakes. Not repulsive like a dirty cow barn, or a fish that's been left out too long. The scent was more nauseating and unsettling, as if something was forgotten in the cellar long ago, and you still can't quite put your finger on what it was and where it is to clean it up.

Unfortunately, since Mrs. Chaipul was the caterer and owned the only kosher restaurant in Chelm, no one dared bring up the subject. You didn't want to get on her bad side. Once, a traveler from Smyrna had mentioned that the noodle kugel was a bit dry, and he had been chased from the restaurant with a frying pan.

But now that Mrs. Chaipul had married Rabbi Kibbitz, (she kept her own name, but that's another story) some of the villagers decided that perhaps it was time to broach the subject.

It was a week before Chanukah when the rabbi heard a knock on the door of his study. He looked up from his reading and saw four of Chelm's finest citizens, standing nervously with their hats in their hands. There was Reb Gold, the cobbler, Reb Kimmelman, the world traveler, Reb Cantor, the merchant, and Reb Stein, the baker.

Rabbi Kibbitz welcomed them in.

In a matter of minutes, the story was presented. As much as they loved Mrs. Chaipul, Reb Cantor said, her latkes made everyone sick. Even though her famous matzoh balls were as heavy as lead, they were still delicious, but no one looked forward to nibbling on her latkes.

"And worst of all," added Reb Stein, "she always piles the plate so high! You don't want to offend her by not eating them all, but for the next three days... nothing tastes good."

The rabbi nodded his head wisely. He knew exactly what they were talking about. Over the years he had developed a trick of hiding several of the latkes in his pockets and then slipping out the back door to feed them to a goat. But he shrugged, "What do you suggest?"

"Well," said Reb Kimmelman, "you're married to her. You could bring it up."

"Tactfully," said Reb Gold, "of course."

"You're right," the rabbi agreed, shaking their hands. "There is nothing that a husband and wife should not be able to talk about."

He was wrong.

That evening, Rabbi Kibbitz brought up the subject, and his wife slammed the door in his face. Literally. She locked him out of the bedroom, and he had to spend the night curled up underneath the kitchen table, shivering with cold.

"What have I done?" the rabbi moaned that night, and for the next seven evenings. "Is my marriage ruined? Who can the rabbi talk to when he has problems?"

The night of the Chanukah party arrived. Rabbi Kibbitz, stiff and exhausted, was not at all interested in attending. After the evening prayers, he went for a long walk. He was seriously considering skipping the whole affair and crawling into bed for a nap before his wife came home and kicked him out. Still, he was the village rabbi, and his place was with his congregation.

So, he stood in front of the doors to the social hall, and steeled himself for the ordeal that was to come. You see, the rabbi especially did not like the smell of his wife's latkes. They always reminded him of the embarrassing odors that wafted from his aunts when he was a child. Finally, he opened the door, stepped in, and held his breath for as long as possible.

At last, gasping and feeling faint, he was forced to inhale.

What was this? He didn't feel sick. He breathed again, deeply this time. His nose twitched like a bunny's. He sniffed the air. Something actually smelled good. Not revolting and disgusting, but rich and delicious. He turned to the stove in the kitchen, and much to his surprise saw Mrs. Rosen, the washerwoman, and her daughters, laughing and frying latkes as if they had done so forever. There was a line for the latkes, and the rabbi noticed that as soon as the villagers got their plates filled, they scurried to the back of the line, and ate standing up while they waited for more.

"Good job!" said Reb Gold, patting the rabbi on the back.

"Best latkes ever," agreed Reb Stein.

"Come," said Reb Kimmelman and Reb Cantor, taking the rabbi by the arms and leading him to the front of the line. "You deserve to eat some of these."

The Rosens piled the rabbi's plate high with the most perfect golden brown latkes he had ever seen. They were thin and crisp and delicate, with just a light sheen of oil.

Everyone watched as he cut into one, and lifted the fork toward his mouth. From this close, they smelled even better—like the warm sun of summer made alive once again in the midst of winter.

Just as Rabbi Kibbitz was about to close his mouth, he saw his wife watching him from across the room. Her face was frozen, expressionless.

The rabbi bit in. The latke melted in his mouth. He chewed it slowly and thoughtfully. At last he swallowed, sipped some water, and spoke.

"Very good." He smiled. Mrs. Rosen hugged her daughters. "Still," he continued, "I like my wife's latkes better."

There was a moment of astonished silence, and then all at once the social hall filled with laughter at the rabbi's wonderful joke.

No one noticed when Rabbi Kibbitz set his plate down unfinished and sneaked out, back to his house, where he crawled into bed for a nap.

He awoke when he heard the front door shut. Grumbling, the rabbi began to get himself ready to sleep under the kitchen table.

"Stay," said Mrs. Chaipul putting a hand on her husband's arm. "Mrs. Rosen's latkes are better than mine. I asked her for the recipe, and tomorrow she's going to show me. Still, it was sweet of you to say that you liked mine best." Then she kissed her husband on the cheek.

"But I do," said the rabbi.

Mrs. Chaipul laughed and closed her eyes.

The funny thing was, Rabbi Kibbitz thought, he really did like his wife's latkes better. True, they tasted awful and smelled worse, but they had always been made with love. Her love. And for him that was the most delicious flavor in the world.

# We Need a Miracle

At the end of the sixth day of Chanukah everyone in the small village of Chelm was scurrying home to light their menorahs at dusk.

Just before the sun set, mothers and fathers would gather their children in the darkening house, and the shammos candle would be lit from the cooking fire. Then, with blessings and song, the shammos would be used like a match and another candle would be lit! On the second night, two, on the third, three, and so on until on the last night of Chanukah eight candles burned brightly (plus the shammos candle, which didn't really count).

Oh, how the children's faces twinkled as they spun their dreidels in front of the flickering lights! Even in the midst of winter, there was cause for joy and feasting.

It was on the sixth night that a problem was discovered.

Little Doodle, the village orphan, had spilled a box of Chanukah candles on the floor of the Levitsky house. Ordinarily, this would not be a problem. Every year Doodle ate his latkes with Reb and Mrs. Levitsky, whose children had grown up and moved away. Everyone knew that Doodle was a bit of a klutz, so if he knocked over a box of candles, it was no big deal.

However, as he picked up the candles from the floor, Doodle began to count. This was something he was learning in school, and was getting very good at.

Martin Levitsky watched the young boy with a smile. "So, Doodle, how many candles are left?"

"Nine," said young Doodle proudly.

"Very good." Reb Levitsky patted the boy's head. Then he frowned. He looked at the menorah, with its seven candles—six plus the shammos—burning.

"Chaya," he called to his wife. "How many days of Chanukah are left?"

"That's easy," Doodle said. "Two!"

"He's right, Martin," answered Chaya Levitsky as she brought another platter of latkes from the kitchen.

"So, how many more candles do we need?"

They all thought for a moment. Seven plus eight plus one plus one.

Doodle answered first, "Seventeen!"

"Right again," smiled Mrs. Levitsky. "A latke for reward."

"But we only have nine candles," said Reb Levitsky. "Doodle, are you sure you didn't lose any? Maybe they rolled under the table?"

"No." The boy licked his greasy fingers. "I picked them all up."

They searched the entire house, but in the end the answer was the same. Only nine.

"Don't worry, Martin," said Mrs. Levitsky, "Your heart can't take it. Tomorrow, we will borrow some."

The next day, Reb Levitsky went early to the synagogue. He searched the cupboard where the boxes of Chanukah candles were normally stored, but found it was completely empty.

So, he went upstairs and knocked timidly on the door to the rabbi's study.

"Ahh, Martin," said Rabbi Kibbitz. "Would you happen to have any spare Chanukah candles? For some reason, Mrs. Chaipul and I are almost out."

"I was about to ask you the same question," said Reb Levitsky.

Just then, Reb Stein, Reb Cohen, and Reb Gold raced into the rabbi's office.

The three friends explained that they were all running out of Chanukah candles, and so were every one of their neighbors!

"How many do you have?" the rabbi asked.

They looked in their boxes and counted again. Reb Stein and Reb Gold had eight. Reb Cohen had nine. No one had more.

"The manufacturer must have made a mistake!" said Reb Cohen. "What will we do?"

"This is indeed a problem." Rabbi Kibbitz stroked his long beard. "But we all have enough candles for tonight, do we not?"

Everyone nodded.

"So, we will send Rabbi Yohon Abrahms to Smyrna to borrow or buy some more candles."

Everyone laughed! A solution had been found. The schoolteacher was summoned, classes were cancelled, and he climbed on his horse, and rode off on his mission to Smyrna.

Later that afternoon, the villagers gathered in the round square to greet Rabbi Abrahms and collect their candles.

Half an hour before sunset, when the younger rabbi's horse finally appeared, the whole crowd cheered. When he dismounted, however, his face told another story.

"There are no extra candles in Smyrna," the rabbi said. "And none in any town within a day's ride. I've been riding all day, and oy is my tuchas sore."

The village was distraught.

"We have only enough candles for tonight!" said Reb Gold. "What shall we do?"

"Relax," said Rabbi Kibbitz, raising his hands. "So, we'll light tonight's candles. Chanukah is based on the miracle of oil that lasted eight days. It won't be too difficult for our candles to last an extra day."

Such a wise rabbi! Chelm was relieved. They all went home, lit the candles, said the blessings, ate their dinners, and watched for the miracle.

But, one by one, in every house in Chelm, the candles burned down. At last, the whole village was left in darkness. They all went to bed, cold and afraid.

---

The next morning, the synagogue was in chaos. Everyone was shouting. Even wise Rabbi Kibbitz looked dazed. Each family had brought their empty or mostly empty Chanukah candle boxes to the shul. Someone suggested writing a letter to the manufacturer, but another pointed out that, this year, it wouldn't help. The arguments lasted all day. Never before had the village of Chelm been faced with such a dilemma.

Young Doodle, who was afraid that it was his fault, that he had caused the problem, watched sadly as the grown-ups shouted and bickered. Slowly, he backed out of the synagogue, but in the process, he knocked over the huge pile of candle boxes, which fell to the floor with a clatter.

Everyone turned and stared.

Doodle wanted to run away and cry, but he knew that the right thing to do was to pick up the boxes and the few candles that had spilled onto the floor.

It took him a good ten minutes. The crowd watched frowning and silent. At last, the pile was rebuilt.

Reb Levitsky patted the poor boy on the head, "So, Doodle, how many candles did you find this time?"

"Nine," the boy sniffled. "Only nine."

A disappointed ripple went through the crowd. Nine. Just nine candles for an entire village! Oy.

Then, Rabbi Kibbitz slapped the table beside him with joy. "Nine! That's all we need! We'll light the menorah in the synagogue. Every family will come. It is indeed a miracle!"

That evening, the entire village of Chelm squeezed into the synagogue, as if it were the holiest of days.

They all said the blessings as Mrs. Chaipul lit the shammos. They watched as she handed young Doodle the shammos. A moment later, all eight lights (plus the shammos) were burning brightly.

It was indeed a miracle.

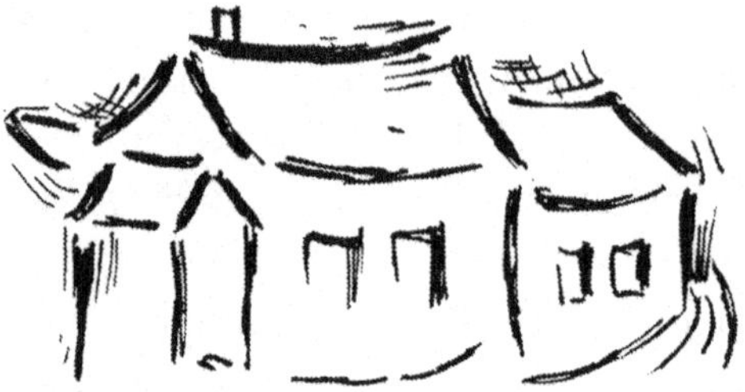

# Rabbi Kibbitz's Surprise

It happened before he married Mrs. Chaipul. It was the year Rabbi Kibbitz lost all of his weight.

He had been huge. As a bachelor, Rabbi Kibbitz had lived alone and had eaten everything that anyone cooked for him. In a community filled with Jewish mothers, all of whom were fabulous cooks, this was a problem. He had gotten bigger and bigger until he was gigantic—exceptionally well fed by Mrs. Chaipul and the rest of the Sisterhood on the fatty foods he loved.

But when the rabbi went to the railway station in Smyrna to buy a ticket to a rabbinic conference in London, England, the ticket master shook his head and said that he was too fat. It would take two tickets just to guarantee him a comfortable seat.

There wasn't enough money in the educational fund for two rabbis to travel.

Rabbi Kibbitz was determined to go to this conference. He bought the ticket, and told Mrs.

Chaipul, "Nothing but parsley, dry bread, and chicken soup with the fat skimmed until I can fit on the train."

"And so he shrunk," as Reb Stein, the baker, liked to say, "from a round New Year's challah to a skinny Sabbath braid."

The whole village walked all the way to Smyrna to see the rabbi off in his baggy clothes. There were hugs and kisses, and lots of farewell tears.

And then, just as the train chugged out of Smyrna, a small scrap of paper fluttered to the ground at Reb Cantor the merchant's feet. It looked like it must have been pinned as a reminder to the inside to the rabbi's coat.

Reb Cantor and the whole village chased the train. The forgetful rabbi was very flattered by the attention. He waved back, and in a minute or two he was gone.

The villagers of Chelm gathered around Reb Cantor as he looked at the note.

"What does it say?" said Reb Gold, the cobbler.

"Because the rabbi is going to England, it's written in English," Reb Cantor said. "Fortunately, I can read English. But the note is ripped. It must have been torn from the pin. It says, 'Bring      It for the Chanukah party.'"

"Bring     It?" everyone said.

"Yes, '      It,'" Reb Cantor said. "Part of the paper is missing."

"No it's not," said Mrs. Chaipul. "That makes perfect sense. LT stands for Lettuce and Tomato. For the rabbi's health salad."

16

"Nonsense," said Rabbi Yohon Abrahms, the schoolteacher, as he examined the note. "There clearly are letters missing. Obviously, the rabbi means bring geLT for the school teacher."

"Maybe it means bring guiLT," said Reb Gold, "like on Yom Kippur."

And the debate began.

For a whole month, while the rabbi was gone, the village prepared for the annual Chanukah party and wondered what they were supposed to bring. The English dictionary in the synagogue's library was consulted until its pages were almost falling out. There was talk of little else.

"Laundry ticket! Maybe LT meant his laundry ticket!" said Mrs. Rosen, the washerwoman. But she checked her racks and found that the rabbi had taken all of his now-oversized clothing with him to London.

" LT?" muttered Reb Levitzky in his sleep. " LT!"

"What do you think the rabbi meant?" the school children asked each other. But no one knew.

The eighth night of the festival of lights arrived, and Rabbi Kibbitz still hadn't returned from England. According to the ticket master, the train had been delayed.

The party was going to have to begin without the rabbi.

One by one the people of Chelm arrived at the synagogue's social hall. And as each new person walked through the door, everyone else looked to see what they had brought.

Mrs. Chaipul, of course brought her health salad. Rabbi Abrahms, the schoolteacher, brought a few gold pieces, hoping that everyone else would follow his example. Reb Gold looked very depressed, and wore all black. "I haven't done anything wrong," he said, waving a finger in the air, "but I brought my guiLT."

But those were not the surprises.

Reb Levitzky wore a plaid skirt. "It's a kiLT," he said defensively.

Some fashionable women took the opportunity to wear fur coats. "Doesn't Mrs. Levitsky have a nice peLT?" A number of the men wore their best beaver hats, convinced that the rabbi meant feLT.

Bulga, the fisherman, brought a strange toasted cheese and seafood sandwich. "I invented it this week," he said. "I call it a smeLT meLT."

The citizens of Chelm had mined the English dictionary from A to Z, and had brought every conceivable variation on the mysterious letters LT. There was a bag of siLT, a sack of saLT, and young Joel Cantor even came dressed as a suLTan.

In fact, most of the children came in costumes. They explained that they were all dressed as various "aduLTs."

The dreidel spun, and the eight Chanukah lights burned brightly in the huge village menorah. Everyone avoided the latkes, and had a glorious time.

It was just before the younger children were to be sent off to bed that Mrs. Chaipul noticed the rabbi had finally arrived. He was shuffling into the back of the social hall. He looked tired. Without telling anyone, she escorted him to a chair and brought him a salad and a plate of non-fat potato latkes. These potato pancakes were an odd shade of grey. The rabbi sniffed them, and said that he had been so cold in London. Being skinny wasn't all it was cracked up to be. Mrs. Chaipul understood. She nodded, and brought him a plate of brisket and kasha varnishkas with gravy.

His arrival wasn't a secret for long.

"Rabbi Kibbitz is here!" a shout went out. "Rabbi Kibbitz! Rabbi Kibbitz what did you mean?"

The ruckus was incredible as every man, woman and child in Chelm called out their interpretation of the rabbi's mysterious note.

"Did you really mean fiLTer?" "What about buiLT?" "SpeLT!" "No, maLT!"

Rabbi Kibbitz, who of course knew nothing of the madness his departure had caused, was puzzled until Reb Cantor, who favored "occuLT" and was wearing a magician's party cape and hat, explained the dilemma.

"We found this note," he said, producing it as if by magic from thin air. "It's torn. Tell us, what did you mean by 'Bring        lt for the Chanukah Party.' What is this 'LT'?"

"What did I mean?" Rabbi Kibbitz wondered, scratching his head. "Hmm...."

"Tell us! Tell us!" the people chanted.

The rabbi raised his hand for silence. "This is a wonderful party," he said. "You've all been so inventive!

"You know, perhaps the rest of the note is still inside my coat," he said as he slid his chair back from the table where he'd been eating. He slowly stood up.

And then...

You remember that Rabbi Kibbitz had lost so much weight? Well, while he was in London, he had lost even

19

more. So, he had taken the safety pin from his coat (the very same pin that had once held the note), and he had used it to take in the waist of his pants.

The pin had suspended his trousers for weeks, but after such a feast, the poor pin gave up.

So, as Rabbi Kibbitz stood up in front of the entire village of Chelm, the safety pin popped out, and all of a sudden the famous rabbi's trousers fell down to his ankles.

There was a hysterical uproar of embarrassed laughter in the social hall.

The learned rabbi looked down in astonishment.

"Now I remember!" he said, laughing along with everyone else. He shrugged, "When I was in London, I was supposed to buy a new beLT !"

It was a truly uplifting festival of light.

# A Cold Day in Chelm

It was a cold day in Chelm. It was so cold that when Reb Cantor, the merchant, sneezed without covering his mouth, his mucus solidified and blew a hole through the window of his shop, which his wife fixed by throwing a cup of tea at his head. He ducked, and the tea hit the windowpane and froze into place. It was that cold.

It was so cold that the flame of the eternal light in the synagogue froze solid. Instead of flickering brightly, it stood still, like red and yellow glass.

The villagers were frightened. It was just before sunset on the last night of Chanukah. Soup froze on its way from the pot to the table. Vodka oozed as it was poured into its glass. Chanukah candles snapped at the slightest touch. Reb Cantor's matches broke into splinters. Stoves were almost useless. Warm challahs froze into rocks in seconds. Axes had to be warmed or else when they struck the firewood, the blades shattered as if they were made of crystal. The Bug River had frozen solid, trapping in its icy clutches a late flock of geese.

It seemed as if the end was near. Everyone was hungry. They were afraid to go outside because the wind sucked the heat from their skin. The air itself left their lips numb. Kissing could be dangerous. The day had been dark and cold and the night would be darker and colder. Meals were uncooked and uneaten. Chanukah candles, set in their menorahs, were unblessed and unlit. Families stayed in their homes, huddled together in bed.

Even in the house of the wisest man in the village of fools, the menorah was dark.

Rabbi Kibbitz shivered in his bed with his wife, Channah Chaipul (she kept her maiden name, which as you know is another story). The two of them lay fully dressed beneath four sheets, three blankets, two quilts, and seven coats—everything warm that they owned. Still, his teeth were chattering. For the first time in his life, he regretted not owning a dog or a cat.

"Channah," the Rabbi said. "We have to light the candles."

"You do it," she said. "I'll watch from here."

"My hand is too unsteady. The shammos will blow out. You are better at that sort of thing."

"I'm almost warm," she said. "You do it."

"I'm nearly frozen," he answered.

"So? You want me to get out of bed, light the candles, and come back in with icy cold feet?"

He shuddered. The last time she had put a cold foot on his ankle, his heart had nearly stopped.

He sighed and closed his eyes. Maybe in a few minutes he would…

"Are you awake?" she said, elbowing him in the ribs.

"Channah!" he said, suddenly sitting up. "I had a dream!"

"Are you crazy? Lie down, you're letting in a draft."

"No, Channah, I've had a dream. Quickly! Get up! We need to gather everyone in the synagogue."

Mrs. Chaipul squinted at her husband. She hadn't seen him this excited since he'd beaten Rabbi Abrahms, the schoolteacher, at canasta. "What did you dream?"

"I can't tell you," he answered. He slid out of bed and gasped as the frigid air slapped his neck like an icy wet towel. "Tell everyone to bring their menorahs and come to the synagogue. Quickly!"

Grumbling and shivering, Mrs. Chaipul stood, and nearly stopped right there. She wondered if it was possible for blood to freeze. Then, the rabbi went one way, and his wife went the other, banging on doors and windows. They ran as fast as they could, (which was remarkably briskly, considering their ages) waking villagers and telling them to gather in the synagogue.

"What? Why? Are you crazy?"

"Yes," said Mrs. Chaipul. "But the rabbi has had a dream. So you can freeze in your house or freeze in the shul. It's up to you."

Parents groaned. Children were wrapped in blankets. Doors were pried open. Menorahs were carried carefully, lest they crack into pieces on the short trip to the synagogue.

The small shul filled quickly.

Rabbi Kibbitz stood at the front, on the bimah, with five tallisim wrapped around his shivering old shoulders. He stood beneath the eternal light, staring at the still frozen flame.

"Is everyone here?" he asked. Everyone looked around and nodded. No one was missing. "Then, please, somebody shut the door!"

"It's shut," came a shout from the back.

"Oy," muttered the chilled rabbi.

"So, Rabbi, what is it?" said Reb Cantor. "What is so important that you asked us to risk life and limb to come to synagogue on a night so cold my eyeballs almost froze?"

"I had a dream," the rabbi said.

"So, I heard," answered Reb Cantor. "You maybe want to tell us what the dream was?"

"I dreamed," Rabbi Kibbitz sighed, "that all the villagers of Chelm gathered together in the synagogue."

"Yes? Yes?"

"Well, in my dream, it was a cold, cold night, and the Chanukah candles weren't yet lit."

"Yes? Yes?" the villagers repeated.

"And everyone, all of you, came here to the synagogue."

"Yes? Yes?"

The wise rabbi shrugged. "That's it. We were all here. Then Channah nudged me and I woke up."

"That's not much of a dream," muttered Mrs. Chaipul.

The citizens of Chelm stared in disbelief at their beloved rabbi.

"You're crazy!" shouted Reb Cantor. "You yanked us out of our moderately warm beds and dragged us here to tell us that you had a dream that we were all here? That's it! Rabbi Kibbitz has finally lost his mind! Rabbi Abrahms, it is time for you to become the chief rabbi of Chelm."

The villagers began to grumble and argue and stamp their feet. A wave of exasperated hot air lifted to the ceiling as their voices rose into shouts.

"Wait, wait!" Rabbi Kibbitz said. "Please, listen."

Just then a thin child's voice shouted, "Look! Look!"

It was young Doodle, an orphan and one the most foolish boys in the village of Chelm.

Doodle was pointing up at the eternal lamp. The pale light was thawing—flickering faintly, but growing brighter as it filled the synagogue with its glow of red, orange, yellow and gold.

Reb Cantor himself lifted Doodle up. "Careful, careful now," he whispered, as the young boy touched a shammos to the light of the eternal flame.

That candle was passed back and forth throughout the shul, as every family lit their own shammos. Everyone held their breath, wondering whether the wind and the cold would extinguish the thin flames.

Then, at long last, the villagers of Chelm said the blessings all together. The shammosim touched the other candlewicks. Soon, for each family one flame became eight (plus the shammos).

Now the synagogue was full of light, and the villagers began to sing.

Reb Cantor swept the old rabbi up in a bear hug. "That was some dream!"

Everyone laughed and danced.

They stayed there all night, and the candles burned so slowly that it was well past dawn before the last one burned out.

That morning, when the doors to the synagogue were opened at last, a warm breeze left the shul and spread out over the village.

The ice on the Bug River cracked, and the flock of trapped geese took flight. All the villagers watched and cheered as the birds sped south.

And from the east, the sun rose higher and its rays felt warm with promise.

# The Chanukah Duck

---

**M**ost families in Chelm, the village of fools, kept farm animals. Geese, chickens and ducks were for eggs; sheep were for wool; goats and cows were for the milk. These animals were often treated as part of the family. They ate the same food as their owners, and they slept inside the house during the long, cold winters. Sometimes the animals were given names, and when they passed away, they were mourned deeply (before being eaten).

Not the Gold family. The Gold family was too poor to keep animals. Reb Gold was a cobbler, and a good one. The shoes he made and repaired lasted for years, which unfortunately meant that he didn't get a lot of repeat business. Every bit of money he earned was spent on food and clothing for the family. Wood for the fire was cut from the Black Forest. There was no extra money to feed an animal. Even if there had been money, there was no room in the house. Joshua and Esther Gold had

27

six children. The five oldest were boys named David, Jonah, Micah, Eli, and Abe. The youngest was a girl, and she was the favorite. Her name was Fegi Shoshana and everyone called her "Little Bird."

"Daddy, why don't we light the candles now?" Fegi asked on the first night of Chanukah. "Everyone else in Chelm already has candles in their window."

Her mother sighed. "Little Bird, we don't have any Chanukah candles."

"We have Sabbath candles. Can't we light them?"

Esther Gold looked at her husband. Joshua Gold shrugged. "Why not?"

So the whole family gathered around as the Chanukah blessings were sung and the Sabbath candles were lit.

"But what shall we do for candles tomorrow night?" whispered Esther Gold to her husband. "And what will we do for candles for the Sabbath? Those were our last two!"

"Shh," he answered, quietly. "We'll worry about that tomorrow. Look how happy they are."

The two parents smiled together as they saw the faces of their children bathed in the warm glow of the candles.

"What about dreidels?" Fegi said. "All my friends say they play a game called dreidel."

Again her mother sighed. She looked at her husband. "You tell her."

Her father frowned. "Little Bird," he began, but just then he was interrupted by a tap-tapping at the door.

"Who could that be?" David, the oldest son, wondered.

"I'll get it!" Fegi said, brightly. She ran to the door and opened it. "Look! It's a duck!"

"Nonsense," Joshua Gold said. "What would a duck be doing at our house in the middle of the night?"

"In the middle of winter!" agreed his wife.

"A duck?" David said. "Really?" All the brothers turned toward the door.

"Come in, come in," Fegi urged.

In waddled a duck. It was a white duck with bright orange feet and a bright yellow bill. Strangest of all, balanced on the flat part of the duck's bill was a shiny brass dreidel.

With great care, it hopped up on the dinner table, and dropped the dreidel next to the merrily burning candles.

"Quack-key!" it said.

"Thank you, Reb Duck!" answered Fegi. "Mama, may we keep him?"

It took every ounce of Esther Gold's self-control not to snatch the dirty bird off her nice clean dinner table.

All the children clamored for an answer.

"I don't know if we can afford keep him," their father finally managed. "But of course the duck is welcome to stay for the night."

"Quack-key!"

The children clapped their hands, and soon the dreidel was spinning merrily. It was a wonderful night, and when it was time for sleep, the duck hopped onto Fegi's bed, and lay down beside her.

"Quack-key!" it said quietly, before tucking its head under one wing.

After the children were asleep, Joshua and Esther Gold were whispering to each other.

"We can't eat the duck, can we?" Joshua asked his wife.

"Of course not," Esther answered sharply. "The duck is our guest. It even brought a gift."

"How did a duck get a dreidel?" Joshua wondered. "Where did it come from?"

"How should I know?" Esther replied. "Probably it is lost."

Her husband sighed. "Probably it is some nobleman's duck, and that is his dreidel, and tomorrow they will arrest us all."

"Sha!" said Esther Gold, making a sign against the evil eye. "Go to sleep."

The next morning the duck was gone, and Fegi was in tears.

"You didn't…" Esther accused her husband.

"I didn't!" Joshua Gold raised his hands. "I promise."

They searched the house. The brass dreidel was still on the table, but there was no sign of the white duck.

That afternoon, Joshua took the dreidel to the house of Reb Cantor, and told the merchant the whole story.

"A Chanukah duck?" Reb Cantor said. "That's a good story and it's a nice dreidel. May I buy it from you?"

Reb Cantor knew that the Golds were always in need of money, so he offered a good price.

Joshua Gold sighed, and nodded. He took the money and used it to buy candles for Chanukah and for the Sabbath, and a new wooden dreidel for the children.

That night, the children were hushed as the blessings were sung and the Chanukah menorah was lit. As soon as the second light was burning brightly, Fegi ran to the door and opened it to the dark dark night.

"Reb Duck?" she called. "Reb Duck?"

Her father put a hand on her shoulder. "Shut the door Little Bird. You're letting the cold in."

With no duck and only a wooden dreidel, the evening was dismal. The Gold family went to bed early.

Now, it was the tradition in the Gold house to eat fried potato latkes only on the last night of Chanukah. The parents claimed that it was what their families had always done, but everyone knew that the real reason was because they didn't have enough money for potato pancakes every night. Still, one night of latkes was better than none, and everyone looked forward to the celebration.

But shortly after breakfast on the seventh day, Fegi tripped over the sack of potatoes that had been brought out for the latkes, and there was a horrible snap in her left arm. Reb Gold carried his daughter to Mrs. Chaipul, the rabbi's wife, who also served as the village midwife and doctor. Mrs. Chaipul worked her magic, gave Fegi a soothing tea, set the broken arm back in place, and wrapped it tightly in plaster.

The cobbler carried his daughter back to their house, and breathed a sigh of relief as she fell into a deep sleep in her bed. Then he collected the sack of potatoes and took it to Mrs. Chaipul.

She tried to wave him away. "Nonsense. It was nothing. You don't owe me anything."

But Reb Gold refused to take charity when he could pay. At last she was forced to accept the potatoes, and Joshua Gold trudged home, sad and dispirited.

That night, despite her injury, Fegi woke and leaped out of bed just as the blessings were sung and candles were lit. Her family hugged her tight.

"I want a latke!" Fegi said, merrily.

"Little Bird, Little Bird," Esther Gold moaned. "There are no…"

But just then she was interrupted by a tap-tapping at the door.

"Who could that be?" David, the oldest son, wondered.

"Reb Duck!" Fegi said. She dashed to the door and opened it with her one good hand.

"Quack-key!"

"Come in, Reb Duck. Come in!" Fegi clapped her hands in delight.

In waddled the duck. It was a white duck with bright orange feet and a bright yellow bill. Strangest of all, the duck was dragging behind it a sack of potatoes.

"This is a most unusual duck," Joshua Gold said. "Not that I'm complaining."

Fegi knelt down and gave the duck a one-armed hug. "Thank you, Reb Duck."

All the boys cheered.

The duck said, "Quack-Key"

"Mama," Fegi said, brightly. "Reb Duck says he would like a latke!"

"Quack-key!" agreed the duck.

"Little Bird," Esther Gold said. "I'm sorry. We can't."

The room was instantly silent.

"And why not?" Joshua Gold demanded. "The duck brought us potatoes."

"But no eggs," Esther Gold wailed. "I didn't think we were going to have latkes, so we ate our last egg for dinner. You can't make latkes without eggs. They fall apart."

Fegi frowned, but she realized the truth of her mother's words.

She looked sadly at the duck and told it, "I'm sorry, Reb Duck. We can't have latkes. If you want to take back your potatoes, you can."

The duck sighed.

(Later on, Joshua Gold would swear to everyone that the duck really did sigh.)

It hopped onto Fegi's bed, nestled itself onto her pillow and loudly said, "QUACK-KEY!"

The Gold family watched as the duck's eyes grew wide and wild. "QUACK-KEY! QUACK-KEY!"

Suddenly, it flapped its wings and flew right at them!

The Golds were shocked. They jumped back in fear. Everyone panicked and screamed, except Fegi.

She just started laughing. "Look," she said, pointing to her bed. "Reb Duck is not a he-duck. He's a she-duck!"

There, nestled on her pillow was the largest duck egg they had ever seen.

"QUACK-KEY!" the duck insisted.

What could Esther Gold do? She took the egg. She shredded the potatoes. She cracked the egg and mixed it into the batter. While the potato pancakes fried the children spun their wooden dreidel. Every so often the duck would say, "Quack-key," and Fegi would giggle.

At last the latkes were ready and the first to be served was the duck.

Later that night, after everybody was full and the children (and the duck) were snoring, Joshua Gold whispered to his wife.

"When a duck eats its own egg is it cannibalism?"

"Sha," she whispered back. "Don't spoil it."

The next morning, Mrs. Duck was still there. She stayed with the Golds and slept on Fegi's bed for the rest of her very long life. She never again brought dreidels or potatoes to the Gold house, but everyone who tried her eggs swore that they tasted just slightly of latkes.

"Quack-Key!"

# A Present? For Chanukah?

I want a Christmas present," little Shmeenie Schlemiel said as she tugged on her father's coat.

Jacob Schlemiel, the carpenter, looked up from his Sabbath studies. "A what?"

"A Christmas present," Shmeenie said firmly.

Jacob smiled. His daughter was almost five years old and already she had the determined look of her mother.

"And where is your mother?" he asked.

"Off with Abraham and Adam visiting friends."

Jacob nodded and frowned. "Where did you hear about Christmas presents?"

"In Smyrna," Shmeenie said. "I was playing in the market with a girl named Alexandra, and she told me about all the gifts she was going to get. You wouldn't believe how many gifts she's going to get! I don't want that many presents, just one."

"Just one?" Jacob scratched his head. "Sweet one, I don't like to tell you things like this, but Jewish people don't get Christmas presents."

Shmeenie's face wrinkled into a frown. She nodded, thought for a moment, and then said, "All right. I want a Chanukah present."

"A Chanukah present you want?" Jacob was stunned. Who ever heard of such a thing! "My tiny one, Chanukah is not a holiday for presents. We Jews give gifts on Purim. Now on a birthday you might get a present. And your birthday is coming up on the last night of Chanukah."

"I know," Shmeenie nodded. "But I want a present before that. I want a Chanukah present."

"No," Jacob shook his head. "I don't think so." He returned to his reading.

"Christians get Christmas presents," Shmeenie said. "Why can't Jews get Chanukah presents?"

Jacob peered at his daughter. "If all the Christians jumped off a cliff, would you also jump off a cliff?"

"No," Shmeenie said. "But I don't want to jump off a cliff. I want a Chanukah present."

Jacob almost laughed. But this was serious.

"If we were wealthy, I would," he said at last. "We are not. Where would the money for this gift come from? You want to eat less food?"

"What about the tsedaka box?" Shmeenie said, pointing. "You put money in there every day."

"But that is for others who are less fortunate than us."

"So they can buy presents instead of us?"

"No, no," Jacob said. "For food and shelter. Some people aren't as lucky as we are to have so much."

Shmeenie stamped her foot. "This summer, I saw you give Reb Stern a whole bunch of money. And then I saw him buy a ball for his son."

Jacob sighed. So young, so observant. "When I give money to Reb Stern, I don't make conditions. It is up to him to use it however he thinks best."

It was clear that this argument wasn't holding water either.

"Besides, if I bought a gift for you, I would have to buy gifts for your twin brothers."

"So? What's wrong with that?" Shmeenie smiled brightly. "And Mama needs a new apron, too."

"We don't have enough money!" Jacob snapped. "No Chanukah presents! Enough! End of conversation." Jacob slammed his book shut, stood up, and then sat back down. "You made me lose my place."

He didn't have to look to know that his daughter was crying. In fact, it was better that he didn't look, because if he saw her tears he knew he would promise her anything. And he couldn't. Already there wasn't enough.

Shmeenie stood for a moment, the tears running down her cheeks, and then when she saw her father wasn't going to change his mind, she turned and ran into her room, slamming the door behind her.

Jacob felt miserable. When Rebecca and the boys came home, he mumbled an apology and went to bed early.

But Shmeenie Schlemiel was persistent. She didn't mention it again to her father, but she pestered her mother and her brothers with her idea that everyone in the family should get presents for Chanukah. They all just laughed and said no. Impossible!

"What's so wrong with Chanukah presents?" she wondered aloud one day as she walked through the streets of Chelm. "Gifts are wonderful things!"

"Yes," said a voice. "Gifts are wonderful things."

Shmeenie looked up and saw Chaya Levitsky, the synagogue caretaker's wife.

"That's exactly what I've been trying to tell my family," Shmeenie said. "But they don't understand. They keep telling me that there is not enough money. And even worse, that nobody gives presents for Chanukah. I just want to know why!"

Chaya Levitsky nodded. "Does your family love you?"

"Yes."

"And do you love them?"

"Absolutely."

"So, who needs gifts?"

Shmeenie looked at Mrs. Levitsky and patiently explained. "People don't need to give gifts. People want to give gifts."

"So you should give gifts," Mrs. Levitsky said.

"But I don't have any money." Shmeenie said, exasperated.

"Ahh. So now you know how your family feels."

"But..." For a moment the little girl looked as if she was going to cry. Then she composed herself. "Do you want to know the truth? I don't really want to give gifts. I just want to get one. Just a little doll."

"I understand," Mrs. Levitsky said. "Do you know what they call a gift that is an obligation?"

Shmeenie shook her head.

"Taxes." Mrs. Levitsky laughed, patted Shmeenie on the head, and walked off.

Frustrated, Shmeenie stomped her feet in the snow for a good five minutes, and then she had an idea...

On the first night of Chanukah, after the candles were lit, while the latkes were frying and Adam and Abraham were spinning their dreidels, Shmeenie sneaked off to her room.

Jacob and Rebecca exchanged nervous looks, but neither said a word.

A few moments later, the little girl came back with a small bag.

"Everyone, come here!" she said brightly. "I have presents for you."

The family gathered around, and from the bag, Shmeenie took out four scrolls of paper and tied with hair ribbons. She solemnly handed them out.

As one, the Schlemiel family slipped off the ribbons, unrolled the papers and read:

> My gift to you
> Is love from me
> It doesn't cost much
> And it's given for free
> It will never run out
> Or go away
> That is my gift
> For you today.

You have never seen so many tears of joy in one room.

A moment later Abraham and Adam and Jacob and Rebecca ran from the room. In another moment they were back with little gifts of their own—small dolls made from scraps of cloth and pieces of wood. Even Jacob gave Shmeenie a small seven-sided doll house with real windows and doors that opened.

The laughter from the Schlemiel house that evening filled the entire village of Chelm with joy.

"Chanukah presents, who would have thought?" Jacob Schlemiel said to his wife just before bed. "Let's just not make a habit of it...."

# The Challah That Ate Chelm

The baker of Chelm had a new apprentice named Muddle, and he was a disaster. Everything he baked went wrong. The light rye came out brown, the dark rye was orange, the pumpernickel swirl looked like a candy cane, and the challah... oy! One week it was lopsided, the next flat, one week it was square, and another the braids were a tangle of yarn.

"Maybe you should become an artist," Reb Stein, the baker, said one day while they were taking inventory.

"Why, because I'm so creative?" Muddle answered, dropping a sack of flour at Reb Stein's feet.

"No," said Reb Stein, "because you can't seem to do the same thing twice."

"I'll think about it." Muddle smiled. "That's the last bag of flour."

"The last bag of flour?" Reb Stein yelped. "That's impossible!" He jumped up and searched the storeroom from top to bottom.

"What's the big deal?" Muddle asked. "So, we order more flour."

"It's not so simple, Muddle," Reb Stein tugged his beard. "Tomorrow is the first night of Chanukah. That means it's almost Christmas and New Year's. My flour suppliers are going to be as slow as snails about refilling my stock. We have only enough flour to make challah for one night! You see why that's a problem?"

Muddle nodded solemnly. "Yes. I forgot to buy Chanukah presents."

"Oy, Muddle!" said Reb Stein, shaking his head.

"What we need is a miracle," Muddle said, cheerfully. "Like the eight lights of Chanukah."

"Let me tell you something," Reb Stein said. "Miracles are like spinning a dreidel, sometimes you get everything, but mostly you get none. Now, let's mix the dough so it can rise overnight. We'll worry in the morning."

So, Muddle and Reb Stein began to blend the flour, water, yeast, salt, sugar, oil, and eggs to make the Chanukah challah.

"Maybe we should add extra oil to the recipe," Muddle suggested, "to celebrate the miracle of Chanukah."

Reb Stein patted Muddle's shoulder, "Listen, Muddle, it's all right to add a little extra oil, as long as you add a little extra of everything else to make up for it. Keep in mind, though, that we've only got so much flour. Got it?"

With that, Reb Stein forgot who his apprentice was, took off his apron and went home.

Muddle, however, had an idea.

"What makes the bread rise?" Muddle asked himself. "It's the yeast. We've got plenty of yeast!"

So, Muddle took an entire sack of yeast, mixed it with water and sugar, waited ten minutes, and then added the bubbling mixture to the challah dough.

It took hours to knead the slippery dough, but by four in the morning, he was done. He covered the huge vat with a sheet. Then he took off his shoes and lay down on the counter for a nap before morning.

---

"What's he doing here?" said one voice.

"What's that thing pushing him down the street?" said another.

"Who cares?" said a third. "Run!"

Muddle opened his eyes, and was surprised to find himself rolling like a barrel down the middle of Chelm's main street, with something pushing at his back every time he slowed.

It's a dream, he thought, closing his eyes, until suddenly with a bump, Muddle hit a rock and was launched high into a tree. He grabbed onto a branch and hung on for dear life. Of course by then, he had reopened his eyes. What he saw was incredible.

The main street of Chelm was covered with a deep white goop. Villagers were cowering in doorways, or peering out of windows. The ooze was growing and spreading and getting bigger still!

From his perch, Muddle could see the goop seeping through the entire village. It seemed to be originating from the windows and doors of Reb Stein's bakery.

This is a silly dream, Muddle thought. He reached over to pinch himself, and he fell right into the muck. It smelled like dough. It tasted like dough.

That's when he realized it was no dream.

The yeast! The bread! It had risen and was rising still. It was flooding into Mrs. Chaipul's restaurant and climbing the walls of the butcher shop. It chased Rabbi Kibbitz down the street, until the rabbi ran into the synagogue and struggled to push the door shut behind him.

From his bedroom, Reb Stein heard the noise. He looked out the window, and roared, "Muddle! The challah has escaped! Do something!"

So, Muddle grabbed the edge of dough that was nearest and began lifting it. "Help me!" he yelled to the people of Chelm. "We've got to braid it!"

One by one the villagers joined in. They grabbed the dough and they pulled. They tugged and twisted, pounded and pushed.

The gigantic challah dough was slippery. It wriggled and fought back. At one point, Muddle found himself suspended fifty feet above the dirt street. Still he held on, rolling the dough into a braid as it reluctantly submitted to the teamwork of an entire village.

"Into the oven!" Muddle shouted.

With wagons, mules, horses and their shoulders, the people of Chelm somehow managed to stuff the challah into Reb Stein's largest outdoor oven.

Exhausted, Muddle leaned against the wall of the bakery.

"What about the second rising?" Reb Stein asked, shaking his head.

Muddle gasped. He looked at the oven. "Everybody run away!"

In a moment the streets of Chelm were deserted. Everyone hid under their beds and waited. Muddle, who had no bed, climbed back into his tree, and covered his ears.

Twenty minutes passed. Forty minutes passed. The oven was shaking.

And then "BROUCH!" The oven exploded! Pieces of bread flew everywhere! One chunk even knocked Muddle out of his tree.

When he awoke, Muddle found himself lying on the bakery's counter.

"Oy," he mumbled, rubbing all the sore spots on his body. "What a dream!"

Just then Reb Stein burst into the room. "That was no dream," he said, sternly. "Your challah broke my biggest oven!"

"I'm sorry, Reb Stein." Muddle stared at his feet. "Maybe I shouldn't be a baker."

"Maybe not," Reb Stein agreed. "Fortunately, the bread tastes very good, and there seems to be enough of it to last for the rest of the week. The people have taken up a collection of Chanukah gelt to establish you in whatever business you like, as long as it's not baking."

Muddle looked at the pile of money on the counter in astonishment. "So," he said, "it was a miracle."

"Muddle," Reb Stein warned, "Don't push your luck."

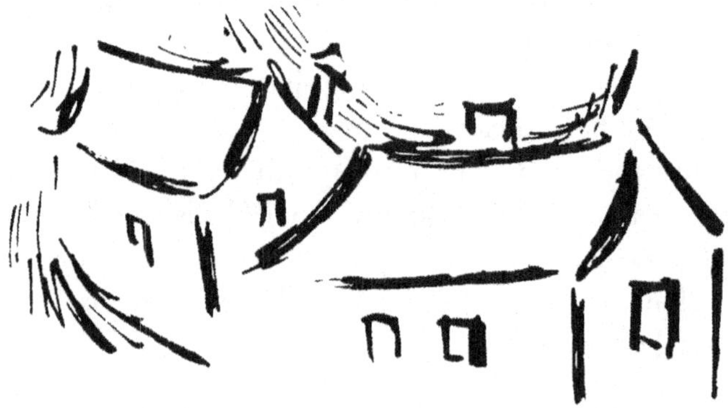

# What a Gift!

By now, nearly everyone has heard of the Eastern European village of Chelm, known far and wide for its doltish "Wisefolk." Far fewer are aware of the nearby village of Smyrna, which was equally well known for its practical jokes, usually at the expense of the citizens of Chelm...

The three pranksters from Smyrna arrived in the small village of Chelm on the morning before the first evening of Chanukah with a large package. Doodle, the village orphan, ran along side the wagon, shouting, "Look! Look!" The young boy made such a noise that everyone within earshot came out into the round square to see what all the commotion was about.

On top of the cart sat the largest, most gigantic round box that had ever been seen. It looked like a hatbox big enough for an elephant's bowler. The three pranksters from Smyrna stopped their horse, and with a great deal of struggling unloaded the package, which was completely covered in gold and silver and black paper.

Mrs. Chaipul, who owned the kosher restaurant, was the first to approach the three men. "What's this?" she asked.

"We have heard that you in Chelm have a new custom," said the first prankster. "Giving gifts for Chanukah!"

"So, we have brought you a gift," said the second prankster.

"What is it?" Doodle said eagerly.

"Well, we wouldn't want to give away the secret," smiled the third. "But since you asked, we have brought you *All the knowledge in the world!*"

*"All the knowledge in the world,"* the other two Smyrnans repeated.

They spoke the words with deep sincerity, and then all three pranksters burst into laughter.

Their giggles were infectious. They became chortles and then belly laughs. The dozens of Chelmfolk who had gathered by now all joined in. Such gaiety!

At last, as the laughter died down, Rabbi Kibbitz stepped forward and formally addressed the three pranksters. "We thank you for this kindness, and apologize that we have nothing to give you in return."

"Quite all right, quite all right," said the pranksters.

"Nonsense," said the rabbi, who was known as the wisest of all the wise folk of Chelm, "We must give you a gift as well."

"Come to our Chanukah party!" said Mrs. Chaipul, "It will be on the last evening of Chanukah. You can share our latkes, play dreidel, and by then…"

"By then," blurted Reb Stein, the baker, "we will have finished wrapping your present, which will be as wonderful for you as *All the knowledge in the world* will be for us."

The three pranksters quickly accepted the invitation before they again disintegrated into guffaws, which started everyone else laughing again. By the time the villagers of Chelm recovered, the pranksters had vanished down the long road to Smyrna.

"That's really *All the knowledge in the world?*" wondered Reb Gold, the cobbler.

"It is an awfully big package," said Mrs. Cantor, the merchant's wife.

"Nicely wrapped, too," said Reb Cohen, the tailor.

"I was just going to invite them over for a nice dinner," said Mrs. Chaipul, frowning at Reb Stein. "How in the name of the prophets are we going to give them something better than *All the knowledge in the world?*"

"I'm sorry," said Reb Stein. "It seemed like a good idea."

"Well," said Rabbi Kibbitz, "we'll think of something."

---

For the next seven days, all the wise men and women of Chelm discussed the gift that they would give to the good people of Smyrna. They became so excited that they completely forgot to open their package.

"Our gift should be big," said Reb Gold, the cobbler. "At least as big as theirs."

"Bigger!" echoed Doodle.

"And nicely wrapped, too," added Reb Cohen, the tailor, who had already taken its measure.

"Their gift is quite light," said Reb Stein, who had given the round box a nudge, and found to his surprise that it moved easily. "Our present must be just as nice as their gift to us."

"Nicer than *All the knowledge in the world*?" Mrs. Chaipul snapped at Reb Stein. "How is that possible?"

"Now, Channah," chided Rabbi Kibbitz, "be pleasant."

"Pleasant?" Mrs. Chaipul said. "You want pleasant? Find me a present that's nicer than *All the knowledge in the world*. Then I'll be pleasant. Maybe I should cook up a big batch of latkes."

All the gathered villagers turned pale and shuddered at the thought.

In the meantime, Jacob Schlemiel, the carpenter, and Rabbi Yohon Abrahms, the school teacher, set to work building a new box to contain their marvelous gift—whatever it was going to be. They increased the tailor's measurements by ten percent, and with a great ruckus of hammering and sawing, constructed an even bigger square wooden box, with a spring-loaded lid.

"Watch this!" said Jacob Schlemiel. "The lid is hinged, like a bear trap!"

He demonstrated how a simple pull on a rope opened the box, and then another pull closed it with a loud BANG!

"Such an amazing box!" said Reb Cohen, the tailor, "I have just the right drapery to wrap it with—a bolt of silver and white silk, like a tallis."

By then it was the evening of the seventh day of Chanukah, and all of the festival preparations were in place, save one crucial detail.

"What will we put inside the box?" asked young Doodle.

The villagers of Chelm fell silent before their larger but still empty crate. Jacob Schlemiel pulled on the rope, opening the box once more, but the thrill of the invention was gone. One by one the villagers drifted away, and not even wise Rabbi Kibbitz had any good ideas. "Maybe it will snow," he mumbled. "A box full of snow might be a nice gift."

---

Just before dawn the next morning, the whole village of Chelm was awakened by a loud BANG!

The startled roosters began crowing. The dogs began barking, and everyone in the village got dressed and hurried to the round square, where the three Shimmel sisters, who ran the dairy farm on the outskirts of Chelm, stood beside the gift box, obviously surprised at the sudden crowd.

"My goodness!" said Reb Gold, as he pushed on the square box. "It's gotten much heavier!"

"I'll get the wrapping!" shouted Reb Cohen, running back to his shop.

"What if it caught a bear?" said Reb Stein.

"Nonsense," said Mrs. Chaipul. "It's not moving." But both she and Reb Stein kept a wary eye on the package as Reb Cohen returned with his wrapping cloths.

"Excuse me, Rabbi," Bertha Shimmel began, "but we, that is to say my sisters and I…"

"But nothing!" Rabbi Kibbitz exclaimed. "We have been provided with a miraculous gift for the town of Smyrna! Let's not question our luck."

If anyone had been looking at the Shimmel sisters, they would have noticed a series of guilty glances, but the rest of the villagers were too busy congratulating themselves on finding an appropriate gift and preparing for the evening's festivities.

When afternoon came, the pranksters from Smyrna arrived, along with many other grinning Smyrnans. The sun set, the candles were lit, and the party began. There was wine and challah, latkes, apples, cheese from the dairy farm, and wonderful fish caught and smoked by Bulga, the fisherman. Everyone sang and danced around the menorah, until at last Rabbi Kibbitz announced that it was time to open the presents.

Such a hush fell over the crowd. All the villagers from Smyrna appeared nervous, except the three pranksters, who chuckled in quiet expectation.

Little Doodle, since he was the first to see the gift, (and it was already past his bed time) was allowed to cut the wrapping paper and open the round box. He did so with glee, shredding the beautiful gold and silver and black paper in an instant.

Then, with the help of Rabbi Yohon Abrahms, Doodle lifted the lid, and peered inside.

"It's empty!" Doodle shouted, his voice echoing hollowly in the depths of the box.

"What?" "How?" "Impossible!"

Everyone from Chelm rushed forward to peek into the empty box.

"*All the knowledge in the world* has escaped!" shouted Reb Stein.

The three pranksters fell to the ground laughing, while the rest of the Smyrnans looked guiltily at the large silk-wrapped square box that the villagers of Chelm were about to give to them.

"Where did it go?" asked Mrs. Gold.

"What will we do?" echoed Reb Cantor.

Rabbi Abrahms, the schoolteacher, shrugged and muttered, "I'm not sure something so valuable belonged in a box in the first place."

Finally, when they all agreed that the cardboard box was indeed empty, the villagers of Chelm gathered and with sad expressions faced the Smyrnans.

"We seem to have misplaced your gift," said Mrs. Chaipul diplomatically. "I'm sure it will turn up. And when it does, we'll be sure to enjoy it. Thank you so much."

By now, the three pranksters were howling with laughter as they rolled in the dirt. Eventually, though, they pulled themselves together enough to get up, dust themselves off, and sputter, "You're welcome."

"Please," said Rabbi Abrahms, "open our gift to you."

Reb Cohen whisked away the beautiful drapery, revealing the giant wooden box. Rabbi Abrahms handed the pranksters the rope to open the lid.

"What do you suppose it is?" whispered Mrs. Chaipul to Reb Stein.

The three Shimmel Sisters glanced at each other with silent shrugs.

The first prankster pulled on the rope, but nothing happened. Then two of them tugged, and still it did not open. Finally, all three pranksters together yanked on the rope with all their might.

There was a crick and a crack, and instead of the lid popping up, all four sides of the box split open.

The three pranksters leaped back quickly enough to avoid the wood, but not the deluge that followed. For out of the large box spewed an immense flood of cow manure!

The ripe bovine dung oozed over the three pranksters, covering them from head to foot in brown and pungent muck!

What a shock! What an insult! All and one were stunned silent, until little Doodle began to giggle and then laugh at the sorrowful expressions on the poor men's faces. With the ice broken, the villagers of Smyrna joined in, and then everyone was laughing at the absurdity, even the pungent pranksters,

Finally, the hilarity faded and Bertha Shimmel stepped forward with an explanation. Once a month, when the pile of refuse outside their cattle pens grew too large, the Shimmel sisters heaped the dung into a cart. They brought the load into the village to fertilize all the gardens.

For years, people had complained about the horrible smell, so when Bertha Shimmel saw the immense box, she immediately assumed that it was for their use and they had filled it to the top!

With that, Bertha and her two sisters burst into tears.

"There, there," said Rabbi Kibbitz, comforting the three women. "There is no need to cry. Without fertilizer, the crops will not grow. Through you, the village of Chelm has provided Smyrna with the *Gift of Life!*"

"Listen," said the Mayor of Smyrna, stepping forward sheepishly, "about that empty box..."

"Empty box? Nonsense!" said Rabbi Kibbitz. "As soon as young Doodle opened your gift, *All the knowledge in the world* filled each of us. Now we must study together to understand its meaning."

Even the villagers of Smyrna were struck silent by such unexpected wisdom from the little village of Chelm. The party broke up quickly after that, and the three pranksters, who had to load the smelly gift from Chelm onto their cart, were the very last to leave.

# The Chanukah Business (Part One)

Once a week in the village of Chelm, Reb Cantor, the merchant, and Rabbi Yohon Abrahms, the schoolteacher, went for an early morning walk. They met in the village square when it was still black, squinting up at the sky as the sun crept up, inch by inch, over the Black Forest, and off they'd tramp. Rain or shine, snow or mud, one morning a week, it was their habit.

For Rabbi Abrahms it was a chance to get a little bit of exercise and clear his head before spending the rest of his day inside trying to teach a horde of youngsters, most of whom would much rather be out running in the fields.

For Reb Cantor, who awoke muttering and stumbling about the house in the dark, complaining bitterly under his breath, exercise was fine, but this was mostly a chance to pick the brain of the man who was almost certain to succeed Rabbi Kibbitz as the chief rabbi of Chelm. Not that the legendary elder rabbi was going anywhere soon, (Reb Cantor made a sign against the evil eye) but it was better to be prepared.

One warm dry autumn morning, the two men were in high spirits as they made their way along the trail beside the Bug River.

"Tell me," Reb Cantor asked. "What do you think of Chanukah?"

"I like latkes," Rabbi Abrahms grinned. "Are you inviting me to your house already?"

"Of course you're invited," Reb Cantor smiled back. "But what do you think of it as a holiday?"

Rabbi Abrahms shrugged. "Not much. It's not in the Torah. The Book of Maccabees is fascinating. It's nice to know that every so often Jewish people win a battle. Why do you ask?"

"Well," Reb Cantor hesitated. "Ever since the Schlemiels invented the Chanukah present, people have been buying things from me to give as Chanukah presents."

"So?" said Rabbi Abrahms, stopping to pick up a stone, which he skipped three times across the narrow river before it stuck in the mud with a thunk. "That sounds like a good business."

"It is!" Reb Cantor agreed. "It seems to be almost a third of my local business right now, and it keeps getting better every year. I got a letter from my cousin Richard in America. He wants to start selling Chanukah presents too."

"Again, so?" This time the rock skipped only twice before sinking.

"So, Richard wants to trademark the phrase 'Chanukah Present' so that we can make some money every time somebody calls something a Chanukah present."

Rabbi Abrahms began trotting up the side of East Hill. "Can you do that?"

Reb Cantor sighed and jogged after the young rabbi. "In America, you can trademark anything. You can sell anything. Especially around Christmastime."

"I'm confused," said Rabbi Abrahms. "I thought we were talking about Chanukah."

"Yes, that's the point," Reb Cantor said, panting. "Chanukah would not be a present-giving holiday if it wasn't so close to Christmas."

Rabbi Abrahms tugged his short beard. "I see."

"So, you understand my problem?"

"No."

The chubby merchant stopped for a moment to catch his breath and then sputtered, "Chanukah is not much of a holiday. That's my point. Should we be giving gifts just to keep up with the Joneses?"

Rabbi Abrahms looked puzzled. "Who are the Joneses?"

"They are a Christian family who live next door to my cousin Richard in Brooklyn. They give their children presents. Richard's children heard about Chanukah presents and now they want some also. But since Chanukah lasts eight nights, his children want eight presents. And it's not that much of a holiday!"

"There's a miracle and there's latkes," Rabbi Abrahms said. "What more do you need for a holiday? Come on, I want to get to the top of West Hill, too."

"Oy!" Reb Cantor groaned. "I'm having an ethical problem, which as a businessman is likely to cost me money. I can make a lot of money selling Chanukah presents. I'm just not sure I should."

Rabbi Abrahms grinned. "So you have a conscience after all."

Reb Cantor smiled back. "A little one. I just think that we have to be careful sometimes. The next thing all the children will be wanting a Chanukah bush."

"So, what's wrong with a Chanukah bush?"

"It's not Jewish." The merchant gaped at the young rabbi. "It's like a Christmas tree."

"I have a Chanukah bush," Rabbi Abrahms said, softly.

"What?" Reb Cantor stopped in his tracks.

Rabbi Abrahms nodded. "Our family always had a Chanukah bush. But it's not what you think. It wasn't about trying to be like the Christians. It was a tradition about survival."

The school teacher told his story while the merchant walked beside him.

# Rabbi Abrahms'
# Chanukah Bush

When I was a little boy, I loved everything about our Chanukah bush. Long before I moved to Chelm, I lived with my parents and my sister in Russia, in Moscow. Getting the bush was so exciting! A week before Chanukah, we'd go out into the woods and cut down a pine tree just like the Gentile families. During the wagon ride there, my father would hum, while mother sat silent. My sister and I, bundled in furs, would read or doze in boredom. We'd get to the woods, and depending on whether Chanukah was early or late, we'd slog through mud, snow or ice.

Finally we'd find the perfect tree—not too small, not too large. Father would begin hacking with a hatchet, while Mother built a fire to make hot chocolate, and prayed he didn't chop off a foot. He wasn't much of a woodsman. As I got older, Father let me help, which was when Mother stopped watching us. Finally, we'd shout, "Watch out!" and jump back, as the bush creaked and fell.

We would drag our bush to the wagon, lift it into the back, and freeze the whole way home.

We didn't decorate it. Mother didn't want glass balls shattering. No lights either. Mother refused to hang candles because of the fire hazard. Our bush was a little sparse, but still, it was a nice bit of green in the house on dark and cold winter nights.

We had another tradition. On the first night of Chanukah, after the candles and the blessings, Father would break a branch off the bush, and burn it in the fireplace.

The next night, he would light two branches, and the night after that three. Each night he would toss in one more branch, until on the eighth night, he would take his hatchet, cut up and burn the entire tree. Mother didn't really like this, and she stayed in the kitchen making latkes. Then we'd play dreidels and eat hot potato pancakes in front of the burning bush.

As I grew older, I realized that having a Chanukah bush was strange for a Jewish family, but when you grow up with something you don't come right out and question it. When my friends asked me, I sometimes fibbed and told them that my sister was adopted; she was originally Christian and we did it for her.

I finally got up the courage to ask during the Chanukah following my bar mitzvah. It was the last night, and Father had just finished chopping the tree into bits and was feeding it into the fireplace.

I came right out and said, "Father, if we're Jewish why do we have a Chanukah bush?"

"It's because of the Cossacks," my sister said, superior as always. "They would have killed our family if we didn't have a bush. Isn't that right, Father?"

Our father stared into the fire and said, "Well, almost…"

---

Your great grandparents Isaac and Rebecca, may they rest in peace, did not live in Moscow. They lived in a Russian village that was so small it did not even have a name. Once there had been a lot of Jews, but the weather was bad, the ground was poor, and the Cossacks were near enough to put fear into their hearts. One by one the Jews left, until our family were the only Jews remaining.

They were quiet about it. In public, the family spoke Russian and Polish. Only at home did they converse in Yiddish or pray in Hebrew. There was no synagogue nearby, so your great grandfather taught his sons Torah at home by the light of the Sabbath candles and with the curtains shut.

They were forgotten. They stayed because they owned land, a rare thing for a Jewish family. They had a warm two-room house with one feather bed, cots for the children, cows, chickens and potatoes. There wasn't much food, but there was enough, and a bit extra to trade for clothes, nails and candles.

One winter, a regiment of Cossacks moved into the village. It wasn't such a rare thing for soldiers to stay in the homes of Gentile peasants. But when the Cossacks found Jews, they usually preferred to kill them before they ate all their food and slept in their houses.

Fortunately, these soldiers never learned that Isaac and Rebecca were Jews. The other villagers didn't say. Either they'd forgotten, or were kind enough to pretend.

So the Captain of the Cossacks, a large man named Yevgeni moved into Isaac and Rebecca's bedroom, forcing them to sleep in the common room with the children.

Christmas drew near, and the Cossack wondered where was the family's tree?

Isaac had no choice. He took his sons into the forest. Yevgeni came along, picked out the proper pine, and let the peasants do the work.

When the first night of Chanukah came, Isaac and Rebecca could hardly bring out their brass menorahs, light candles and say prayers.

So Isaac plucked a branch from the tree, mumbled something under his breath, and threw it into the fire.

Yevgeni, puffing on a pipe, said nothing on the first, second or third nights. But by the fourth night, his curiosity got the better of him.

"Izzy," he asked, "What are you doing? If you keep that up, there won't be anything of the tree left by New Year's."

Isaac had already thought of an answer. He lied.

He told the Cossack that one winter during his Grandfather's life, when Isaac's father was only a boy, the snow had grown so high that it had covered the windows and blocked the doors. The firewood dwindled until all that was left was the Christmas tree, and so his grandfather had burned it, branch by branch, surviving on the meager warmth its green wood provided.

The captain accepted this explanation with a grunt, and stared into the flames.

Three days later, the Cossacks were called away, and rode off. Few tears were shed in the village. Everyone was alive, although their food stores were diminished. Winter would be harsh.

In Isaac and Rebecca's bed, Yevgeni had left fleas and lice.

That evening was the eighth night of Chanukah, and Isaac took great pleasure in chopping the tree into small bits and feeding it, along with the insect-ridden bed covers, into a roaring fire.

A few potatoes were fried, and for the first time that year, the blessings were spoken aloud and the dreidels spun merrily.

---

When my father finished his story, he asked if I understood. I nodded, and said that when I was married and I had children, in my home, the Chanukah bush would burn brightly.

Father gave me a hug. Mother smiled. My sister rolled her eyes.

But we all watched together as the green pine tree popped and crackled in the fire.

# The Chanukah Business (Part Two)

The merchant and the young rabbi had finally reached the top of the second hill, and the sun was getting higher in the sky.

"So, now do you understand why I have no problem owning a Chanukah bush?" Rabbi Abrahms said. "Do you have a problem with it?"

"No, of course not." Reb Cantor shook his head. "Never mind. But I'm still stuck."

Rabbi Abrahms grinned. "You need to watch out before you step into a mud puddle."

"Not my foot," said Reb Cantor. "My business. What do you think I should do about these Chanukah presents?"

Rabbi Abrahms tugged his beard again. Sometimes he thought that maybe if he kept tugging his beard it would grow as long and luxurious as Rabbi Kibbitz's beard. Mostly though, when he tugged at his beard some of the hairs fell out and it stayed as short as ever.

"Do people enjoy giving and receiving gifts?" Rabbi Abrahms asked at last.

"Of course," said Reb Cantor.

"And you can profit from this?"

"Hoo boy, yes," said Reb Cantor. He was still puffing and huffing from the climb.

"So," Rabbi Abrahms said, "I don't see much of a problem. Sell the gifts, make the money."

"But," panted Reb Cantor, "what about the Christianization of a Jewish holiday?"

Rabbi Abrahms raised his hands, palms up. "What Christianization? On Chanukah you tell the story of the Maccabees. You tell the story of the miracle. You light the menorah. You eat the latkes. You give and get some presents. Where's the Christian part of that?"

"The gifts!" Reb Cantor coughed. "The gifts."

Rabbi Abrahms shook his head. "Do you think that the Maccabees ate latkes on Chanukah? No. Potatoes came from America. Some enterprising potato farmer decided that having potato pancakes was good for business. Who are we to complain? They taste good— except for Mrs. Chaipul's."

Both men paused to shudder at the thought of Mrs. Chaipul's infamously lethal latkes.

They looked down the hill at the village of Chelm below. Bertha Shimmel was already up and on her rounds delivering milk from her family's dairy farm. Now other doors and windows were beginning to open as another morning began.

Reb Cantor sighed. "I suppose you are right. But how can we avoid doing it to excess? If there's one thing the Christians do, they go all out celebrating their holiday. It's crazy-making."

"Last year I went to the Schlemiel house for latkes," said Rabbi Abrahms, licking his lips. "They were delicious. I ate so many that I felt sick to my stomach for three days. You know what? This year, when I come to your house to eat latkes, I'm not going to eat so many. You have to let people learn from their mistakes and set their own limits. Now let's go back."

Without another word, Rabbi Abrahms set down the hill at a jog.

"Wait!" shouted Reb Cantor after him. "Richard also wanted to know how you should spell it in English, 'Hanukkah' or 'Chanukah'?"

But the young rabbi was already far down the hill, and Reb Cantor decided that it probably didn't matter anyway, and set off after him.

# How Joseph Won His Bride
# With the Spin of a Dreidel

J oseph Katz had been practicing dreidel all year. The villagers of Chelm were whispering about it. Even in Chelm, it wasn't normal to spend so much time playing with a toy.

True, Joseph had been born during Chanukah. It was natural for him to play with the four-sided top. But all the time? If Joseph had still been a little boy, that might have been different, but he was a young man of almost seventeen! He should not be living in his parents' house and spinning a clay top from morning until dusk.

Joseph, however, paid them no mind. Every morning after helping his poor mother with her chores, he spread an assortment of dreidels across the kitchen table, and began spinning them. Whenever anyone asked, he explained, "I am spinning the dreidel to win my bride."

Now, in case you don't know, a dreidel is a top with four sides that is twirled at Chanukah time. On each side is a Hebrew letter celebrating the miraculous lights of Chanukah —*Nes Gadol Haya Sham*, or "A great miracle happened there."

On Chanukah nights while the candles burned, the children of Chelm gathered together and spun their dreidels, gambling for raisins, nuts and dates. But in Chelm of course everything was backwards. The letters in Yiddish meant something different than they do to our children. Shin meant "stell" or put one back, and if you spun a Hay, or "halb," you would take half. Gimmel, instead of getting the pot meant "gib," or give everything back into the pot. And Nun, instead of nothing, meant "nimm," or take everything.

Joseph Katz, after years of practice, could spin any dreidel and it would fall on whatever letter he wanted. He was, in modern terms, a hustler, a dreidel shark. He could bounce the dreidel off a glass and still land it on a Nun ten times out of ten. He could spin a dreidel upside down on a plate and when it fell it would always land on Nun.

On his seventeenth birthday, on the first morning of Chanukah, Joseph put his dreidels in his pocket, and strode forth, ready to win his bride.

The early morning customers in Mrs. Chaipul's restaurant were surprised to see young Reb Katz join them. Joseph had never before entered the restaurant without his parents. But, they relaxed when he began spinning his dreidels on the breakfast counter. Some things never changed.

"So, Joseph," said Reb Stein, the baker, "would you like to play a game?"

Joseph shrugged. "I don't have any money."

"I'll wager a copper coin against all your dreidels," said Reb Stein with a smile.

Everyone laughed. Joseph Katz would be lost without his dreidels.

Again Joseph shrugged. "All right, but since I might spin a Hay, you'll need to wager two copper coins."

"Why not?" grinned the baker.

The coins went onto the table. Joseph's dreidels went beside them.

Joseph reached for a dreidel, but Reb Stein put his hand on Joseph's. "No, no," he said. "We'll use my dreidel."

Again Joseph shrugged. "You spin first."

"My children," Reb Stein said, "will love all these dreidels."

He spun. The dreidel twirled and landed on a Hay.

"Halb!" said Reb Stein. He swept half of Joseph's dreidels into his pocket. "Your turn."

Joseph had already picked up Reb Stein's dreidel. He held it in the palm of his hand and felt its weight. Then he squinted at it.

"So, spin already," said Reb Stein. Everyone laughed.

With a casual twist, the dreidel spun off Joseph's fingers onto the counter like a ballerina twirling onto a stage. Everyone in the restaurant gasped. It spun and spun and spun, and at last fell.

"Nun, nimm," Joseph said. "I take all."

"Luck," said Reb Cohen, the tailor. "Let me try."

It didn't take long for Joseph to clean out the pockets of every single customer in Mrs. Chaipul's restaurant.

And that was just the first day of Chanukah. Every day, except the Sabbath, Joseph took on all challengers in the game of spin the dreidel. And, of course, he won almost every time. Soon enough there was grumbling. When a fist fight nearly erupted, Joseph and his dreidels were brought before Rabbi Kibbitz.

"He's cheating," the villagers said.

"No," said Joseph, "it's a talent. I am only winning enough money to win my bride."

Rabbi Kibbitz tugged his beard and said, "This is a matter of money. It is not something for the rabbi to decide. Joseph must go to Reb Cantor, the Merchant."

Reb Cantor was the wealthiest man in Chelm. The people of Chelm smiled at the Rabbi's wisdom. Joseph, too, smiled. Reb Cantor had a daughter, Leah, and Joseph was in love.

---

So, Joseph was invited to the Cantor's house for a dinner of latkes and brisket. The meal was quiet as the young man and the young woman found themselves tongue-tied.

"I hear," said Reb Cantor at last, "that you have been causing a little bit of trouble."

Joseph nodded. "I would like to spin the dreidel to win my bride."

Reb Cantor raised an eyebrow. "Any bride? Perhaps my daughter Leah?"

Both Joseph and Leah's faces turned beet red with embarrassment.

"Would you wager everything you have," said Reb Cantor, "against everything I have? Including my daughter?"

Everyone gasped. Mrs. Cantor's face went white. She clutched at a napkin. "Isaac…" she moaned. "What are you doing?"

"Sha." Reb Cantor raised a hand. "A wager. Joseph, you'll spin. One spin. A Nun wins all. If the dreidel falls on anything else, you give all your winnings to charity and come to work for me. No more of this dreidel nonsense. Is it agreed?"

"Are you sure?" Joseph asked. "I have a talent for spinning the dreidel."

"Joseph, we all have talents," shrugged Reb Cantor. "I am sure if you are sure."

Joseph coughed and nodded. "Agreed."

The two men shook hands. Reb Cantor's wife, Shoshana felt as if she could not breathe.

Joseph took a dreidel from his pocket. He looked at Leah, who blushed and glanced away. He looked at the dreidel and gave it a spin.

It was like a tornado. The dreidel spun fast and furious in a tight circle. For twenty-two minutes it spun in the candlelight. Everyone's eyes were fixed in flickering fascination.

Then the dreidel started to slow. It started to wobble. Everyone leaned forward. Now no one could breathe.

And then, just as the dreidel was about to fall on the Nun, Reb Cantor leaned forward and blew. Whoosh!

The dreidel bumped, tumbled, and fell.

"Gimmel," said Reb Cantor. "Gib. You give everything to charity."

Joseph jumped to his feet. "You cheated!"

Reb Cantor shook his head. "Nonsense. You have a talent for spinning a dreidel. I have a talent for blowing hot air."

Joseph stood frozen. He stared at the old man, and after a long time he nodded.

"You start work tomorrow," said Reb Cantor. "Leah, why don't you pack Joseph up some leftovers for his mother."

While Leah and Joseph went into the kitchen, Mrs. Cantor whacked her husband on the back of the head with a spoon and hissed, "How could you do that? We could have lost everything!"

"Look at them," said Reb Cantor, rubbing his skull. They both watched the two young people whispering in the kitchen. "He's a good one. He works hard. He's kind. If I had lost, I would consider it an early retirement. He would never have turned us out of our house. But I won!"

Mrs. Cantor frowned, saw the way the children looked at each other, and nodded.

And that is how, with the spin of a dreidel, Joseph Katz won his bride.

# Out of the Woods

## *Chapter One*

A sliver of light slid through a chink in the wall and pierced the eyelid of the sleeping Cossack. "Mpf!" he muttered, rolling away.

"Sir?" came a voice. It echoed like a cannon, booming inside his skull. "Vasilly Petrovich?"

"Waa?" muttered the Cossack leader. He groped for a pillow, but instead found himself gripping his lieutenant's leg. "Hmm?"

"The men are hungry," said Ivan Marcovich, Vasilly's second in command. "We have taken all we can from this place."

Petrovich groaned. "What day is it?"

"Midwinter," Marcovich answered, without a trace of irony.

Vasilly Petrovich, Captain of the infamous Lightning Cossack Raiders, sighed and began swimming his way toward consciousness. He had been comfortable and warm under his furs. His dreams had been vivid, and could have lasted all winter. When he was a boy, Vasilly liked to sleep so much that his father had always claimed that his son was descended from a bear. Bears could nap all winter without interruption. Woe befall those who woke a sleeping bear.

He blinked his eyes and stared at the walls of his room on the second floor of the village inn. Rough-hewn logs patched with mud. A rope bed made comfortable only by the goose down mattress he had taken from the local magistrate. His men were sleeping below in the stables with their ponies. Petrovich missed Moscow. He had grown soft there, enjoying warm rooms with walls that did not breathe whispers of winter, drinking water that was almost clean, and eating meals that had both fish and meat at the same table. In Moscow he had been able to sleep until dusk and feast until dawn. Now in the middle of nowhere, he was responsible for his band of twenty men. Sometimes, leadership was difficult.

"What is the next village on the road back to Moscow?" Petrovich asked.

"There aren't any, sir."

"What do you mean, there aren't any?" Petrovich sat up suddenly, and immediately regretted it. The room spun. "We've been heading toward Moscow for a month now. How can there be no other villages on the way? Are we almost there?"

"No. We were going in circles."

"What?" Petrovich's eyes flared red.

"The map reader, Sedoi Miachik, didn't know how to read."

"I'll kill him," the Cossack captain said.

"It's too late," Ivan Marcovich said. "He's already dead."

"Good."

"That is how we know we are lost. We found a new map reader."

"This one can read?"

"Yes."

"And where does he suggest we go?"

"Chelm."

"What?" Petrovich said.

"Chelm."

"Do you have a cold?" the captain asked.

"No. It is the name of the village closest to here that we have not already pillaged. We've been to everyplace else and eaten and drunk everything they had. This Chelm is out of the way, but that means that there should be plenty of food. We could stock our ponies and ride the rest of the way to Moscow on the spoils."

"Really?" Petrovich's face broadened into a smile.

His lieutenant shrugged. "Maybe. None of the men have ever been to Chelm." He hated to tell his leader the truth. With anyone else, he would have lied, but his captain was not kind to those who misled him. The dead map reader was lucky.

Petrovich chewed his lip. "The name rings a bell. Something about Schlemiels coming from Chelm…"

"I don't know," Ivan Marcovich said. "But if we don't go to Chelm, we've got two days ride without any food."

"You mean the men have two day's ride without food," the Cossack captain said warily. "I assume that you have brought me my breakfast."

"Yes, of course. Here it is." Marcovich gestured to a thick ham steak. "But that is the last meat in Smyrna."

Vasilly Petrovich stared at the pork. His stomach was upset. Something was making him uneasy. He had a bad feeling about this Chelm place. Ahh well, it was probably nothing that a good meal and a hard ride wouldn't cure.

Vasilly Petrovich, Captain of the Lightning Cossack Raiders sighed. "Tell the men to get ready."

"They are ready," answered his lieutenant.

"Tell them to pack," Petrovich ordered.

"They are packed."

Petrovich looked at his lieutenant. He looked at the ham steak.

"Tell them to wait."

Ivan Marcovich clicked the heels of his boots together, as he had seen the Czar's troops do, spun around and left his leader.

Petrovich didn't bother with a knife. He picked the slab of meat up in his hands and began to dine.

## Chapter Two

"Rabbi Kibbitz, Rabbi Kibbitz!"

Doodle burst into the elder rabbi's study. Rabbi Kibbitz, the oldest and wisest man in the village of Chelm looked up reluctantly. He was used to the young boy's outbursts.

"What is it Doodle?" Because Doodle was an orphan, the entire village acted like his parents. As a result, no one had taught him how to behave. Or rather, everyone in the village had taught him how to behave, so his mind was a bit jumbled.

"Rabbi Kibbitz! Rabbi Kibbitz!"

"Yes, Doodle?" The rabbi was a patient man; Doodle was just a boy.

"Rabbi Kibbitz!"

"WHAT IS IT?" the rabbi shouted. Enough was enough. Patience was one thing, but he was an old man too, and he might die at any moment.

Doodle jumped, and immediately the rabbi regretted raising his voice. "I'm sorry," he said quietly. "I had too much tea this morning."

"I understand," Doodle said, nodding. "When Mrs. Meier has too much tea, she chases me out of the mikveh with a broom."

"Did you have something to say or did you just want to interrupt my morning?" the rabbi asked.

"Cossacks."

The elder rabbi's blood froze. "No," he whispered.

"Yes," Doodle said.

"Cossacks?"

"Cossacks."

"Oy!" Rabbi Kibbitz rubbed his head. He tugged on his beard. "Really? Where? How do you know?"

"They were in Smyrna. I went to the inn to deliver a letter for Mrs. Chaipul, and I heard them talking. There was a crack in the ceiling, and the Cossack leader's room was just upstairs. They said they are going to come to Chelm and take everything we own. I didn't know what to do. I delivered the letter, and then I stole a pony."

"You stole a Cossack's pony?" Rabbi Kibbitz looked out the window of his study and saw the animal grazing on a few stray bits of grass poking through the snow. To call such a creature a pony was to underestimate its value. Cossack horses were small, but hardy, able to carry heavy burdens and move incredibly fast. It was well known that a Cossack would rather die or lose an arm than lose his pony.

"I was in a hurry." Doodle looked sorrowful. "I didn't know what else to do. I'll give it back."

Rabbi Kibbitz tugged on his hair. He rubbed his skullcap. When he began chewing on his beard he realized that he had to do something and do it quick.

"Good work, Doodle."

"Really? You aren't mad at me?"

"For stealing? I have a little bit of a problem with that. But as you say, you'll give it back." The rabbi stood suddenly, or as suddenly as a man his age could. "Go ring the alarm bell in the square and tell everyone to meet in the synagogue right away. We don't have much time."

Before he had even finished, the boy was gone.

## Chapter Three

"Do-wang!"

The alarm bell in Chelm's round square was a relatively new invention. Reb Kimmelman, the world traveler, had suggested that the villagers could use something like it to warn everyone about danger.

"Do-wang!"

There had been a big fuss, because for years in Chelm there had been no danger, and if you brought a warning bell to the village who was to say that it wouldn't bring the danger with it?

"Do-wang!"

But after dealing with fires, floods, robbers and the Russian army, Reb Cantor, the merchant, had taken matters into his own hands.

"Do-wang!"

He had found the prize in Italy. The bell was to have been set in the tower of the Doge's palace in Florence. It had been dropped by careless workmen, and split in two. Half had been melted down to make bronze statues. Reb Cantor had agreed to take the other half.

"Half a bell will bring half as much trouble," he had argued when he had brought it back to Chelm and hung it from a tree in the round square.

So far, he'd been right. The bell had been silent for years.

"Do-wang!"

Leaning against the tree next to the bell was a heavy iron hammer. Nailed to the tree was a sign that read, "Don't ring the bell! It will only cause trouble."

"Do-wang!"

Little Doodle was nearly exhausted from swinging the heavy mallet.

"Do-Wang!"

## *Chapter Four*

The noise in the synagogue was deafening. Everyone in Chelm was shouting at the same time. Some were blaming Reb Cantor for installing the bell. Some were blaming Doodle for bringing the bad news. Some were just wailing and crying.

"What did we do to deserve this?" one voice said.

"Nothing. Absolutely nothing," answered another.

"We must have done something," said the first.

"Maybe you did," said the second, "but it wasn't me."

"STOP!" bellowed Reb Cantor, screaming at the top of his lungs.

The room fell silent.

The merchant coughed. "Sorry about that, but I have a plan."

Half the villagers cheered. The other half rolled their eyes.

"It's not going to be easy," Reb Cantor said.

"You think it's easy being attacked by Cossacks?" muttered a voice from the back.

"Sha," said the second voice, "listen to what the man has to say."

"Go ahead," said Rabbi Kibbitz, relieved that for once someone else was doing the thinking.

"All right." The merchant stepped up onto the bimah. "As I said, this isn't going to be easy."

"Get to it already!"

Reb Cantor, nodded. "We should run away."

"What?" It was as if everyone in Chelm had the same thought at the same time. "What did you say?"

"We should run away. The Cossacks are going to come. They are going to take our food. Maybe they'll do worse. If we run away, they'll have our food, but at least we're still alive. After they leave, we can come back. They won't stay. They don't know how to farm. All they know how to do is to ride horses and steal. Those are things that we are not so good at. So, we let them take what we have, and when they're done, we'll start over."

Again the synagogue was silent. Absolute silence was a rare occurrence in any synagogue. In Chelm it was even more rare.

Then the objections began, one at a time and all at once:

"They'll be here any minute!"

"I don't have time to pack."

"My great grandfather built my house."

"It's the middle of winter."

"The children have to go to school. "

"Where will we go?"

"How long will they stay?"

"What about my soup?"

Reb Cantor listened for exactly five minutes. The second hand on his watch swept around four times, and when it again pointed at twelve, he raised his hands and shouted, "STOP!"

Then he coughed. If I keep doing this, he thought, I'm going to lose my voice.

"The Cossacks are coming," he said. "We have maybe an hour. Take nothing that you don't need. Take food. Take blankets. Take cooking pots and pans. Don't bring anything extra. Leave your valuables at home. Load your horses. Load your wagons. Load my wagons. Carry sacks on your shoulders. Wear warm clothes and good boots. We will leave in forty minutes. Go!"

There was no more talk. The villagers nodded grimly, and ran home.

Reb Cantor was amazed. "I didn't think that would work," he told Rabbi Kibbitz.

But even the elder rabbi was gone.

## Chapter Five

Thirty-seven minutes later, every single man, woman, child and baby in Chelm were gathered in the round square in front of the small shul.

They had followed Reb Cantor's instructions, and packed as lightly as anyone could when pressed to leave their home at a moment's notice. Tears had been shed over embroidered tablecloths and silver samovars, but nothing inessential had been packed.

Reb Cantor arrived five minutes later, and was scolded by Mrs. Chaipul for missing his own deadline.

"I'm sorry," answered the Merchant. "Who would have thought that so many Jews could be on time?"

"Shall we go?" asked Rabbi Yohon Abrahms, the schoolteacher.

"Let's go," said Rabbi Kibbitz.

"Where?" asked Doodle.

"Oops," said Reb Cantor.

Once again, everyone stared at the merchant.

"What do you mean, 'Oops!'" Mrs. Chaipul demanded.

"I don't know where we should go," the rich man said. "I hadn't thought that far in advance. I'm sorry."

"All right, fine," said Mrs. Chaipul. "There are only two roads out of Chelm, The Great Circular road and the road to Smyrna. The Cossacks will certainly becoming from Smyrna. We will take the Great Circular Road."

"But that goes into the Black Forest," said Reb Cantor. "It's haunted. There is nothing there but wolves and bears, demons and goblins."

"I see something!" came a voice from high up.

Everyone looked up. Doodle had climbed a tree and was staring to the North.

"I see horses. Men. Lots of them."

Mrs. Chaipul put her hands on her hips. "Which would you rather face, bears and wolves, demons and goblins, or a band of Cossacks?"

Reb Cantor rubbed his huge belly. He was beginning to think he'd have a better chance with the Cossacks.

# Chapter Six

Vasilly Petrovich, Captain of the Lightning Cossack Raiders, sat on his pony at the top of East Hill looking down at the village.

"It's awfully small," he told his lieutenant.

Ivan Marcovich shrugged. "Yes, but as far as I can tell it has not been raided by Cossacks in decades. There should be plenty of food."

"It's very quiet," Petrovich said.

Again Marcovich shrugged. "It's the middle of winter."

"Then why are there no fires burning? Why is there no smoke coming from the chimneys?"

Marcovich looked. For this he had no answer. "Shall I tell the men to charge?"

Petrovich grinned. Cossacks lived for the charge. There was nothing like riding at a full gallop into a village, swords drawn. The speed, the thrill, the looks of terror on the faces of peasants. And then, of course there was plenty of fun to be had.

"Yes! Let us ride."

# Chapter Seven

The Cossacks rode down the hill like a windstorm. They were silent at first, but as they thundered closer to the village their voices rose into howls and jeers. At the first cross-roads the group split in three, a perfect formation. The hooves of the horses pounded in the snow. Their breath was like the white gusts of dragons, their yelps filled the streets.

And then, almost as quickly as they had begun, they met up again at the other end of the small village having encountered nothing. No one, no resistance. Emptiness.

They turned their horses around, puzzled.

Their captain's eyes darted to all sides, looking for the trap.

"Quiet!" he yelled.

He listened.

And heard nothing but the panting of the horses, and the stamping of their hooves.

"Well," he said. "That was easy."

## Chapter Eight

"Quiet!" whispered Reb Cantor, the merchant.

They had barely made it into the forest when they heard the riders coming.

All the villagers huddled together in the snow, trying not to make a sound. Mothers soothed their babies.

The Black Forest was silent. Fortunately, the snow wasn't deep, but it covered the ground like a carpet. Ears strained for sound.

"All right," Reb Cantor said, his voice still low. "I think its safe to move on. We won't go too far."

"I know a place," said Doodle.

Everyone looked at the young boy. "You do?"

Years ago, the villagers of Chelm had taken a long journey on the Great Circular road. Days had passed and they had found nothing. To have a young boy tell them that he knew something more than they did was a little bit insulting.

"Yes!" Doodle nodded eagerly. "Not far ahead, off the path is a huge clearing that is covered by trees. It would make a good place to stop."

Rabbi Kibbitz looked at Doodle. "Is it a huge clearing, or is it covered by trees?"

"Both," the youngster answered. "The ground is covered with moss, but the sky is covered with thick trees. I discovered it when I was exploring. I call it the Palace Court of King David."

"Really?" said Rabbi Yohon Abrahms, the school teacher.

"You see," Doodle said grinning broadly, "I do pay attention in class."

The villagers chuckled and moved along. In less than an hour, Doodle led Rabbi Kibbitz, Rabbi Abrahms, Reb Cantor and Reb Gold, the cobbler, off the road, deeper into the Black Forest.

"Are you sure you know where you're going?" Reb Gold asked. He had been invited to see the camp site because Reb Cantor wanted a moment to ask him how the villagers' shoes would hold up on a long march in the snow.

Reb Gold had told the merchant that he made the finest shoes and boots for hundreds of miles. If they were well taken care of, the boots would keep the owners feet dry and warm for days. The sad truth was that many of the villagers' shoes had been neglected over the years. He guessed that the seams would be leaking and the soles damp and cold, and he didn't think they could go much farther.

"We're almost there," Doodle said.

"We can always find our way back by walking backwards in our own footsteps," said Rabbi Abrahms.

At last, Doodle led them into a clearing, and it was just as he had described. The empty space was almost exactly the same size as the Chelm's round square. The ground was remarkably dry, covered in a deep moss. Overhead, branches from huge oak and elm trees acted like a ceiling thick with snow.

Exhausted, Rabbi Kibbitz sat on the ground. "This is more comfortable than my bed at home."

"I'll go get the rest," said Reb Gold.

"I'll come with you," said Rabbi Abrahms. The two of them began walking backwards to follow their own footprints.

Doodle was already gathering wood for a fire.

"You know," Reb Cantor said, "if that snow comes down in the middle of the night we'll all be buried."

Rabbi Kibbitz smiled. "I've always wondered what it would be like to be a snowman. We'll tell everyone to be quiet."

## Chapter Nine

Trying to keep an entire village quiet was like trying to catch a flock of chickens with your hands tied behind your back. In other words, it didn't happen. As soon as the people arrived, the children began to run wild. They had been so good on the sudden and dangerous journey that it was a relief to laugh and dance and sing and shout.

The next problem was where to put everyone. Rabbi Abrahms suggested that they set up their camp sites alphabetically, which Mrs. Rosen the washerwoman, pointed out was very good for him, but not for those whose names came later. Reb Stein, the baker, suggested that everyone be arranged by height, but of course Reb Stein's children were all grown up, and he had no real desire to go to sleep on the ground next to Reb Gold's six youngsters.

At last, Mrs. Chaipul came up with the most logical suggestion. She figured out which direction was north, and told everyone to find a spot in the clearing that corresponded to the location of their homes in Chelm.

This worked out well for everyone except Bulga the Fisherman, who realized that his house, which was on the outskirts of the village put him a good twenty feet into the woods.

Reb Gold invited Bulga to spend the night in his home, saying simply, "Even though my house is small, I've found that we always seem to have room for a newcomer or a guest."

"Besides," whispered his wife to Mrs. Chaipul, "we all have a cold, and our noses are stuffed, so we won't be able to smell him."

If Bulga heard the comment, he ignored it. After all, the cobbler smelled of leather and tanning fluids, so shouldn't the fisherman smell of the sea?

Reb Cantor shivered on the ground, watching the branches for signs of an avalanche.

## Chapter Ten

"The doors were open," Ivan Marcovich told his captain. "None of them were locked. The fires in the fireplaces were out, but the coals were still warm. It seems as if they all just left."

Vasilly Petrovich, Captain of the Lightning Cossack Raiders, sat with his feet up on the village elder's desk. He had shoved all the books and scrolls to one side, and was holding an unlit cigar. "I thought everyone said that the people of Chelm were fools."

"By all accounts they are," Marcovich said. "Their village square is round. The dam on the river is patched with dumplings, and I heard that they once traveled a whole week to move the village before ending up back where they started."

"Why is it so cold here?" Petrovich asked.

Marcovich's eyes darted around the room. "Because you haven't lit the fire?"

Petrovich jumped to his feet and roared. "I am the Captain of the Lightning Cossack Raiders. I have led us to a glorious victory. Am I also to be a charwoman? Find somebody to light the fire."

"That's a bit of a problem," Marcovich admitted.

"Why?" demanded the captain. "Just throw on a few logs and light the fire. There is plenty of paper here to burn as well."

"Because the man with the maps was also the man with the fire."

"What?" Petrovich roared.

"You know that it is dangerous carrying the iron pot with the fire in it." Marcovich stepped back into

93

the doorway, ready to run if his captain's temper grew too hot. "Everyone takes turns. Yesterday it was Sedoi Miachik's turn. When he fell off his horse and died, everyone laughed so hard that we forgot to take the fire from his saddle bag. That was the horse that was stolen."

Petrovich, who had been staring in amazement at the shelves after shelves of books on the walls, spun around. "I thought you said that you found his pony. Open the saddle bags. Take out the fire. Burn some of these books. Do I have to think of everything myself?"

"Yes, we found the horse waiting here for us in Chelm," Marcovich said, "but not the fire pot."

Petrovich stared into the cold fireplace. "Tell the men to start rubbing sticks together. Meanwhile, bring me my furs."

## *Chapter Eleven*

"What do you mean you didn't bring the matches?" Shoshana Cantor asked her husband. She kept her voice down. She didn't want anyone to hear. Especially the children. "If we don't get a fire going soon my feet are going to freeze. Never mind about cooking dinner."

"I wasn't thinking straight." Reb Cantor sighed. "I told everyone only to bring what they needed. I told everyone to leave their valuables at home. Matches are rare. Matches are valuable. So I left all of our matches at home."

"You were the one who told us to bring what we needed. We need matches. No one else will have matches."

"I know! I know!" Reb Cantor said. "I made a mistake. You want to kill me for it?"

"Yes, I do," his wife said. "She looked at his sad and broken-hearted face. "But I won't. Perhaps you should start rubbing two sticks together."

Reb Cantor nodded, and then turned his head. "What's that?"

He sniffed the air.

"It's nothing, it's just smoke," his wife said.

"Yes," said Reb Cantor, "and where there's smoke..."

"...there's fire!" she finished, her face broad with a grin.

They ran out of their house. Well, of course there was no house. They ran out of the spot in the woods that they were calling their house. Reb Cantor was so careless he ran right through the wall. His wife chided him to use the door next time, and he promised he would.

The Cantors made their way through the clearing, careful to stay on the narrow roads that the children had laid out on the moss with rocks. At last they came to Rabbi Kibbitz's house, where Mrs. Chaipul had already set up her huge soup pot and was cooking a broth over a warm fire.

"You have a fire!" Reb Cantor said.

"Yes, of course," said Mrs. Chaipul. "I find that it helps the soup if you cook it over a fire. Otherwise, it's just snow and raw potatoes."

"No," said Shoshana Cantor, "what my oaf of a husband means is, where did you get your fire? Where did the fire come from?"

"Oh!" said Rabbi Kibbitz, his ears perking up. He looked up from a book, and began a sermon, "In the beginning..."

"No no no!" insisted Reb Cantor. Sometimes when the rabbi started talking he could go for hours. "Not historically, where did you get your fire, but immediately. How did you light it?"

"Oh." The disappointed rabbi went back to his reading.

"Doodle did it," said Mrs. Chaipul. She nodded her head. "He said he found it."

The Cantors looked through the walls of the Rabbi and Mrs. Chaipul's house, (they were married and she kept her name—it's a long story) and they saw Doodle running from house to house with a small iron fire pot dangling from a piece of rope.

Reb Cantor strode off after him.

Mrs. Chaipul shouted, "Use the door!"

Reb Cantor caught up with Doodle at the Gold house.

"Use the door!" Esther Gold shouted as he walked through a wall.

"Sorry," he muttered. "Doodle, where did you get that fire pot?"

Doodle, who had just lit the Gold's fire, looked ashamed. His eyes fell to the mossy floor. "It was on the Cossack pony," he said. "In the saddle bag. It was warm and I was cold, so I took it with me. I'm sorry. I didn't mean to steal it. I'll bring it back."

Reb Cantor's glowering face softened. "You mean the Cossacks don't have their fire pot?"

Doodle shook his head.

Reb Cantor smiled. "That's wonderful news!"

"I'll bring it back," Doodle insisted.

"No no!" said Reb Cantor. "Don't do that."

"Yes, yes," interrupted Esther Gold. "Of course you'll bring it back. It's wrong to steal."

"But our enemies are cold," insisted Reb Cantor.

"You want them to freeze to death? If we let them die we're nothing better than murderers."

"I don't want to be a murderer or a thief," said Doodle, and he started to cry. "It's all my fault"

"No no," said Reb Cantor. "They won't freeze. They're in our houses, eating our food. Probably they found my matches, and they're nice and warm."

"Still, Doodle, you must take it back," said Esther Gold. "They may be our enemies, but they are still people."

"Can't he wait until morning?" Reb Cantor begged. "If they're cold over night, maybe they'll leave sooner."

"Excuse me, Mrs. Gold," said Rachel Cohen, the tailor's daughter. The Cohen's house was right next door to the Gold's and the walls were thin. (Actually, they were non-existent.) "I think Reb Cantor's right. Doodle should wait until morning for two reasons."

"And what are these reasons?" Esther Gold said, trying to pretend that she wasn't talking through two walls.

Everyone in Chelm knew that Rachel Cohen was a genius. She was the first girl in recorded history ever to be admitted to the Yeshiva. Some women whispered that she might be as wise as Rabbi Kibbitz.

"First of all," Rachel said, "it's getting dark and we don't want Doodle to get lost."

Doodle nodded his miserable head.

"Second, tomorrow is the first night of Chanukah."

"It is?" said Reb Cantor.

"I forgot," said Esther Gold.

"I didn't," Rachel said. "I brought plenty of candles. Enough for the whole village. Tomorrow night we'll gather together and light the candles, and give thanks. However, we will need the fire pot at least until morning, so that we can make sure that our fires are still burning."

"What do you say?" Reb Cantor asked Mrs. Gold.

Esther Gold sighed. She nodded her head. "All right. But as soon as you can, Doodle, you take that fire pot back to the Cossacks. You're a good boy, not a thief."

"Yes, Doodle," Rachel agreed. "You're actually a hero. Without you, we would have been home when the Cossacks arrived. Without you, we would be freezing in this cold because Reb Cantor forgot to pack the matches."

Reb Cantor's face turned red, but he kept his tongue.

By now, Doodle was feeling better. "I'll see if anyone else needs a fire."

And he was gone.

Reb Cantor too wandered off.

Esther Gold called after him, "Use the door!"

# Chapter Twelve

"Sir?"

Vasilly Petrovich kicked at the dog in his dream.

"Sir?"

He poked his head from under the thick bear fur and glared at Ivan Marcovich. "Vanya," he said. "It better be good news."

The Cossack lieutenant thought a moment and then said, "Mixed."

Petrovich sighed, thought about putting his sword through his lieutenant's heart, and then thought better of it. "What do you mean?"

"The fire pot. It was returned. One of the men found it in the snow outside the Jewish church this morning."

"That is good," Petrovich smiled.

"Yes, but it was empty."

Petrovich frowned. "That is bad."

"Yes, but it means that the villagers can't be far."

"That is good."

"Yes, but it snowed," Marcovich said. "There are no tracks."

"That is bad," Petrovich said. He gritted his teeth. "They are taunting us. Perhaps they are hiding in the cellars of the houses."

Marcovich shook his head. "The floors are all dirt. We've searched all the attics. They are in the woods."

"In the woods? In the winter?" Petrovich laughed. "Then they will freeze. Let them all die."

"But if they have fire and we do not..." Marcovich's voice trailed off.

The Cossack captain had a thought. "Why didn't one of our sentries see the man who returned the fire pot?"

"He was asleep."

"Oh," Petrovich said. "Have him shot."

"It's too late. He froze to death."

Petrovich frowned. "Have him shot anyway. It will be a lesson to the rest."

Ivan Marcovich nodded at his leader. He turned to leave, and then stopped. "Vasilly Petrovich, may I say something?"

"Speak."

"We have already lost two men on this expedition. We are freezing cold. The men are grumbling."

"Have them shot."

"Then it will just be you and I."

Vasilly Petrovich, Captain of the infamous Lightning Cossack Raiders, sighed. He was doing a lot of that lately. He longed to be back in Moscow, listening to poets and watching the opera.

"Tell the men that we will find these villagers, steal their fire, and then kill them all."

Marcovich's eyes brightened. "They are ready!"

Petrovich's eyes rolled. "Vanya, I just woke up. Tell them to wait. I will be there in a little bit."


## Chapter Thirteen

An hour later the small band of Cossacks sat on their ponies in the center of Chelm.

"I don't think they went straight into the woods," Ivan Marcovich said. "They were gone too quickly, which means that they took a road. There are only two roads leading out of Chelm. One is the road to Smyrna, which we came down. We would have seen them if they went that way. We would have seen signs of their footsteps in the snow. The other leads directly into the Black Forest."

Some of the men grumbled and shifted uncomfortably in their saddles. The Black Forest was a place of demons, wolves and bears. Even in the daytime it was not considered a safe place to travel. Even for Cossacks.

Vasilly Petrovich joined his men.

They noticed that he looked rested, well fed and warm. Some of his men thought about complaining, but they also knew that their leader had a temper like a volcano. Maybe that's what kept him warm, they thought.

"Where does that road go?" Petrovich pointed. He had missed his lieutenant's little speech.

"I was just explaining to the men that it goes into the Black Forest, but we don't know where it leads. It's not on the map."

"What about that sign?" Petrovich said, gesturing to the long wooden board shaped like an arrow. "It seems to have a fairly complete description."

"It's in Yiddish," Marcovich said. "None of us can read Yiddish. Maybe it's a warning."

(The sign was a warning, of sorts. It read, "Great Circular Road. It goes a long long way. Nobody knows where.")

"Enough of this," Vasilly Petrovich shouted. "The sign is a challenge! We will ride into the forest. We will find these villagers. The snow will run red with their blood!"

He turned and galloped down the road. His men cheered and followed.

Ivan Marcovich, the Cossack lieutenant, was the last to leave. Cossacks were easy to lead. You told them that there was an enemy and you charged. The men would follow Petrovich over a cliff. It was better, safer, to be in the rear.

## Chapter Fourteen

Rachel Cohen's ears tingled. At first she thought it was the cold, but then she realized it was a sound.

"So," Doodle was saying, "I had never ridden a pony before, but I thought it was time to learn…"

"Shh!" Rachel said. She slapped her hand over his mouth before he could say another word. The two children were in the forest looking for a special bark for one of Mrs. Chaipul's herbal teas. They hadn't realized that they had wandered so close to the road.

They both listened.

"They're coming," Rachel said. "Quickly, run back to the village and warn everyone."

"The village?" Doodle said. "Isn't that where the Cossacks are?"

"Not the old village. The new village. In the woods. Go now. Tell them to be quiet, otherwise…"

Doodle understood and was gone before she finished. He ran like a hare, skipping across the surface of the snow.

In his mind he heard himself shouting over and over and over, "Rabbi Kibbitz, Rabbi Kibbitz, Rabbi Kibbitz."

But when he got to the clearing where the villagers were living, he was out of breath and could say nothing. He couldn't speak.

So, Doodle started jumping up and down waving his hands back and forth and then holding his finger in front of his lips. Up and down. Back and forth. Finger on lips. Over and over again.

"What is he doing?" said Reb Stein, the Baker.

"I think he's gone crazy," said Mrs. Rosen, the washerwoman.

"Poor boy," said Bulga the Fisherman.

At last, everyone in the village was watching.

"I think he's trying to tell us something," said Mrs. Chaipul.

Doodle nodded. Up and down. Back and forth. Finger on lips.

"He's telling us he's crazy," said Mrs. Rosen.

"Maybe he lost his voice," said Reb Cantor.

Rabbi Kibbitz, who was always the last to arrive, watched Doodle and realized. "Oh. He's saying that the Cossacks are coming, and we all should be quiet."

"Oh," everyone said, grinning. It was always good to understand.

Doodle, however, didn't stop jumping up and down, waving his arms and holding his finger to his lips.

"I think," said Reb Gold, the cobbler, "he means now. Right now."

"Oh."

And then, for the third time in recorded history an entire village of Jews fell completely silent.

––––––––––

Rachel Cohen had nearly buried herself in the snow. She had heard all the commotion, and knew that if she could hear it the riders would as well. If she needed to provide a diversion, she would. At last, when the voices of Chelm finally fell silent, she allowed herself a quiet sigh of relief.

Then she waited and watched.

## Chapter Fifteen

The ponies of the Cossacks galloped like a flood flashing along the Great Circular road. Ahead of them the road was clean and white. Behind them a cloud of powder floated gently in the air.

The noise of their charge was like muffled thunder. To the Cossacks the pounding rhythm of hooves on the snowy road was like listening to the first movement of a symphony—a rising resonant compelling call to action, to arms, to battle.

Their horses could gallop for hours without rest. The riders and their steeds were one animal with two heads, four eyes, four ears, and two sets of teeth bared and eager.

They rode and they rode.

Out of one corner of his eye, Ivan Marcovich saw a flash of brown. All alone in the snow. A head? A face? By itself? Nonsense. A rabbit, nothing more.

They rode and they rode.

The Cossack ponies, some said, could ride for a week without pause, but this was not true. It was a lie that the Cossack themselves told to spread fear.

They rode and they rode.

They were getting a little bit bored with all the riding. The road seemed endless. The forest was dark. Black, in fact, which probably accounted for the name. After a while, if you've seen one tree, you've seen them all. And that's all they saw. Trees, trees and more trees. And the road. The endless road. It was flat at least. That allowed their horses to run as if they were on a race track. No uphills, no downhills. Just road, road and more road. Always road ahead, always curving just a little bit to the right.

Vasilly Petrovich, the leader of the Cossacks, was frustrated and exhausted but hadn't been able to think of a good reason to stop the stampede.

And then! And then they saw something new off in the distance. They saw an opening. They saw a house, and then another house.

Petrovich drew his sword.

Behind him all of his men unsheathed their weapons.

For the second time in two days the Cossack band galloped to the attack. Their voices rose in terrifying shouts and spine-curdling screams.

They rode into the village. At the first cross-roads the group split in three, a perfect formation. The hooves of the horses pounded in the snow. Their breath was like the white gusts of dragons, their yelps filled the streets.

And then, almost as quickly as they had begun, they met up again at the other end of the small village having encountered nothing. No one, no resistance. Emptiness.

Petrovich stopped his horse. All of the Cossacks stopped. They fell silent.

"I don't understand," Petrovich said with dismay. "Doesn't anyone live in this part of the world?"

Ivan Marcovich nudged his pony next to his Captain's.

"We're back in Chelm," he said. "We rode in a circle."

Vasilly Petrovich's eyes flashed fire. His sword was already out and he tried to stab his lieutenant, but Ivan Marcovich was ready for this and ducked out of the way. Marcovich held his sword high and faced his captain.

"Sir, has it come to this?"

Vasilly Petrovich, Captain of the infamous Lightning Cossack Raiders, raised his sword to the sky and with every inch of power, every bit of energy, every ounce of frustration and rage, he screamed.

The sound of Petrovich's howl echoed from the village like the sound of blood pouring through streets.

## Chapter Sixteen

Deep in the woods, Rachel Cohen heard the scream and began to cry.

Another village was gone. More people were... She couldn't bear to think of it. She sobbed into her hands, the tears warm against the snow.

At last she rose, and made her way back to the clearing.

When she arrived, she was horrified.

No one was moving. The entire village of Chelm, every man, woman, child and baby had frozen stiff. They stood still in the center of the clearing, like they were locked in ice.

"Mama!" Rachel moaned. She ran forward and hugged her mother.

Rachel was surprised to find that her mother's body was still warm.

Her mother reached down and wiped her child's tear-stained face.

One by one the villagers began to budge.

"Are they gone yet?" Reb Cantor whispered. His back was stiff from standing still for so long.

"I thought..." Rachel covered her mouth and then began to laugh.

Mrs. Rosen shook her head. "Another crazy one."

At last Rachel came to her senses. "Yes, the Cossacks are gone. They rode out of Chelm like the plague. They went to another village. I heard... I heard..."

"There, there," Mrs. Cohen said, soothing her daughter's cheek.

Mrs. Chaipul nodded. "We all heard it. I think that we need some tea."

"We have to go back to Chelm tonight," Rachel Cohen said. "We have to light the Chanukah candles and say Kaddish in our own synagogue. It is the least that we can do for this other village."

Reb Cantor laughed. "So now in addition to being the best student in the village of Chelm you are our General? General Rachel Cohen?"

Rachel looked at the merchant with determination. "What's wrong with a woman leading her people?"

Reb Cantor raised his hands. "Nothing, nothing. My wife does it all the time. Ow!"

Rachel climbed onto a wagon and addressed the villagers.

"We are safe. We are warm. We have food. We have fire. We have family. We have friends. We have spent enough time in the woods. It is time to go home."

With one voice the villagers of Chelm cheered.

## Chapter Seventeen

"Did you hear that?" Vasilly Petrovich said.

"Hear what?" Ivan Marcovich answered.

After dismissing the men, they had returned to the village elder's library to play cards.

"That noise. It's them. The villagers."

Marcovich shook his head, but did not take his eyes off the cards. The captain was known for his ruses. "There are no villagers."

Petrovich threw down his hand and stood. "They are laughing at me. Mocking me."

"Did I win?" Marcovich asked.

"No," Petrovich said, "I won." He moved back to the table and gathered up the collection of foolish four-sided tops that they were using to gamble with. There was no money in this village, no heat. Not much food. What was the point? "Tell the men that everyone will be standing watch tonight. Tell the men that if they fall asleep, I will shoot them before they die."

Petrovich pocketed his winnings and stormed from the room.

Marcovich turned over the cards. "You didn't win," he muttered. "I won."

## *Chapter Eighteen*

The sun had just set. It was so sudden. One moment there was light, and the next it was gone.

The night was black. The Cossack soldiers were cold. Bundled up in every fur they had, they stomped their feet back and forth to keep warm. They could barely see from underneath their fur hats and wool scarves.

The wind blew icy tendrils, biting their eyes with frost. They were hungry and cold and tired.

Each of them knew the thoughts of the rest. They thought of past victories. They thought of hot roasted lamb. They thought of going to bed.

Their captain, Vasilly Petrovich wasn't out here in the icy air. He wasn't freezing with them. He was inside, probably in a bed. Probably warm. Probably asleep.

Some leader. Yes, he had brought them victory after victory, but so what? What did they have? Nothing. They had their furs, which they needed to live. They had their ponies, which every man owned regardless of his leader. A Cossack without his pony was less than a peasant. They had their swords. And what else? Nothing. Little food. No fire.

They missed their wives and their children.

Why were they even here? In the middle of nowhere on the edge of the haunted Black Forest? An empty dead village with nothing to offer.

Feh.

The sky was dark. There were no clouds. The moon was a sliver, but it cast no light. No warmth. The blackness was as deep as the pit of hell.

There were rumors of demons in the Black Forest. There were rumors of imps and devils. A Cossack feared no man or animal, but magic and evil? That was something else.

Perhaps the entire village was haunted. Perhaps they would never leave it alive.

The men shivered, both from the cold and their imaginations.

Which was exactly the moment they saw something shifting in the woods. A movement. It was impossible. There was nothing to be seen.

And then it moved again. Not just one thing. Many things were coming toward them out of the woods.

Eyes. They saw eyes. Bright red eyes. Flickering yellow eyes. Lopsided, moving, dancing. Not the eyes of animals, not people, not wolves, but glowing burning eyes.

They were the eyes of demons. One, five, ten, many many pairs of eyes were coming closer. And closer.

The Cossacks could not move. Their hearts were frozen with fear.

They were brave men. They had fought glorious battles against armies. But armies were made up of men and men could die, but imps and goblins and demons and devils could not.

And those eyes, those bright yellow and red eyes were coming closer. They were coming out of the forest.

The Cossacks had no fire, they had little food, their families were far away. Why were they here?

Without saying a word, it was agreed. The Cossack soldiers ran like children to their horses, they mounted and were gone.

This ride was quiet. The Cossacks did not shout or scream or charge into battle. They slunk away from Chelm defeated, the hoof beats of their fleeing horses muffled in shame and snow.

Ivan Marcovich took a moment to slip into the room where Petrovich was sleeping. He collected his captain's money bag and bade the snoring man farewell.

"Vasilly Petrovich," he whispered. "The men have all left. Demons are coming out of the forest. Good luck."

Marcovich looked around the room for the empty fire pot, but couldn't find it, so instead, he plucked up his leader's sword. He had always admired Petrovich's weapon. The men would believe that he had killed the captain, and they would make him their leader. First he would find a place with a warm fire. He would have to buy the band a new fire pot before they went too far.

He waved goodbye to Petrovich. And then he too was gone.

Toasty and comfortable under his furs in the room full of books, the former captain of the infamous Lightning Cossack Raiders moaned at the bad dream, rolled over, and snored louder.

## *Chapter Nineteen*

"It's amazing," said Reb Cantor as he slid with a sigh into his bed. "I've never said the Chanukah blessings outside before. It was so beautiful walking through the woods with the snow on the ground and all the children holding their chanukias like torches with two flames. In all that wind, I should have thought the candles would blow out. It was a miracle."

"Miracle, shmiracle," said Shoshana Cantor to her husband. "We're just lucky that Doodle sneaked back to the village, borrowed the Cossack's fire pot again, and filled it with coals from our fires before we left our clearing. Otherwise we wouldn't have been able to light the candles at sunset like you're supposed to."

"The little scamp," Reb Cantor laughed. "Of course I would have just gotten some matches from my store room. It's amazing the Cossacks didn't find them."

"You and your matches, Isaac. Give the boy some credit."

"I do," said the merchant. "And Rachel Cohen, too. She was right. It was time to come home. She's a good General. She'll make someone a good wife, ordering him around... Ow!"

## Chapter Twenty

"Rabbi Kibbitz, Rabbi Kibbitz!"

The rabbi opened his eyes. He had just fallen asleep.

"What is it Doodle?"

"There was a man. In your study. A big hairy man. He was asleep. I woke him up. He started waving around a pretend sword. He seemed frightened and cold, so I gave him the Cossack's fire pot. I thought he might be able to use it. A Chanukah present, you know? When I handed it to him, his face went white with fear, and he ran off into the forest."

"Yes, Doodle," Rabbi Kibbitz mumbled, "you are a terrifying young boy. Go back to bed. Good night."

## The End

# Glossary and Notes

Chelm—the village where most of the people in this book live. Also known as the fools of Chelm. A traditional source of Jewish humor. The "ch" in Chelm (and most Yiddish and Hebrew transliteration) is pronounced like you've got something stuck in your throat. "Ch-elm."

Chelmener—the people who live in Chelm. Sometimes known as the wisefolk of Chelm. Often called "The Fools of Chelm".

bar mitzvah—The Jewish coming-of-age ceremony. Celebrated at age 13. Almost always catered.

bimah—the platform at the front of the synagogue where the rabbi stands so that everyone can hear him.

challah—a braided egg bread. In English, the plural of challah is challah.

Chanukah—the festival of lights. Celebrated in the winter, it commemorates the victory of the Maccabees over the Syrians. The miracle of Chanukah was that one day's measure of oil burned in the Temple for eight days. Sometimes spelled Chanukkah. Or Hanukah. Or Hanukkah.

chanukia—the Chanukah menorah. A lamp or candelabra with room for eight candles plus another (shammos) for a total of nine.

dreidel—a four-sided top spun in a children's game during Chanukah. The game of dreidel is usually played for high stakes, like raisins and nuts. Although immortalized in song, rarely are dreidels made out of clay, because clay tops are very difficult to spin. The Hebrew letters on the dreidel are Nun, Gimmel, Hay and Shin. They signify the words, "Nes Gadol Haya Sham" or "A great miracle happened there." In Chelm, where Yiddish is spoken when the game is played, the Shin, means "stell" or put one back. Hay is "halb," so you would take half. But, Gimmel, instead of getting the pot means "gib" or give everything back into the pot. And Nun, instead of nothing means "nimm," or take everything. Confusing, isn't it?

erev—the evening that begins a holiday. Jewish holidays start at sunset and end at sunset.

gelt—money. In the old days, Chanukah gelt was given to teachers. Today gelt means foil-wrapped pieces of chocolate shaped like money.

kasha varnishkas—buckwheat groats with noodles. Serve it with brisket and gravy. Mmm.

knaidel—a matzoh ball dumpling served in chicken soup. Often served during Passover.

kugel—an incredibly rich pudding. Often made with noodles. Mmmm.

latke—a pancake fried in oil. During Chanukah latkes are made of potatoes. During Passover they are made of matzo meal.

mitzvah— a good deed. Not to be confused with a bar mitzvah, which is the coming of age ceremony for boys.

menorah—a candelabra. Usually with seven branches, but on Chanukah it has eight (plus another one for the shammos) and is called a chanukia.

mensch—a good guy. A nice fellah. Kind and generous. You want your daughter to marry one.

matzoh—unleavened bread usually eaten during Passover, the holiday celebrating the Exodus from Egypt. Mix damp matzoh with eggs and fry it to make matzoh brei. Yum!

nachas—joy, pride and happiness. Especially something you get from good children.

oy—an expression of excitement and often pain. "Oy! My back!" or "Oy, I can't believe you're wearing that to a wedding!"

Passover—the celebration of the Exodus from Egypt. Celebrated for eight days. Also called Pesach.

Purim—another holiday involving survival and food. The original gift-giving holiday. Nowadays, presents of food and treats may be given on Purim.

plotz—to explode. As in, "I ate so much kugel I nearly plotzed."

Rabbi—a scholar, a teacher, a community leader.

Reb—a wise man. And, since everyone in Chelm is wise, the men are all called Reb... as in Reb Stein, Reb Cantor and so on.

Rosh Hashanah—the Jewish New Year.

Shabbas—the Jewish Sabbath. Starts Friday at sundown and ends Saturday at sundown. Sometimes called Shabbat or Shabbos.

Smyrna—a village near Chelm. Lots of nice people and a few practical jokers live there.

shammos—the candle used to light other candles on the Chanukah menorah.

shmaltz—chicken fat. Used in cooking and spread on bread. Source of many delicious heart attacks.

shul—the synagogue.

tallisim—plural of tallis. A tallis is a fringed prayer shawl.

Torah—the five books of Moses, the first five books of the Hebrew Bible, which is frequently called the Old Testament.

tsedaka—a gift of charity.

tsuris—woe, trouble, aggravation. Especially something you get from rotten children.

tuchas—the posterior.

Yom Kippur—the day of atonement. No one eats or drinks. No kugel, knaidle, babke, challah or shmaltz. Always followed by the break-fast, a sumptuous meal served immediately after sundown. All the food at the break-fast is devoured in a matter of moments.

yenta—a gossip, a busybody.

yeshiva—the school. In Chelm, the yeshiva is the only school.

## Historical Note

Traditionally, Chanukah is a minor festival that commemorates the victory of the Maccabees over the Greco-Syrians, and the rededication of the Temple in 165 BCE. It begins on the 25th day of Kislev, and continues for eight nights to celebrate the miracle of one day's holy oil burning in the eternal light long enough for more to be made.

*The Books of Maccabees* aren't actually part of the Hebrew Bible. The story of the Maccabees seems to be somewhat historically accurate. The story about the miracle of the oil is found in a section of the Talmud written centuries later.

## Final Note

This book is based on an audio recording that was based on a storytelling tour that was based on a collection of stories written over many years. Those original stories were published in newspapers and magazines around the world. The stories have changed and evolved, they differ from the originals almost as much as the spoken-versions of the stories differ from the written versions.

Thank you for reading this. It has been a pleasure.

—**Mark Binder**
*Pembroke Villa*

## About the Author

Mark Binder is an author, a storyteller, and a nice guy.

His collection, *The Bedtime Story Book* has more than 50,000 copies in print. His first CD, *Classic Stories for Boys and Girls* won both an iParenting Media award and a Children's Music Web award.

The CD version of *A Hanukkah Present*, won a **Storytelling World Honor Award.**

His novel, *The Brothers Schlemiel,* includes many favorite characters introduced in *A Hanukkah Present.*

A former editor of the *Rhode Island Jewish Herald,* Mark loves sharing stories with (and leading workshops for) audiences of all ages in theaters, schools, shuls, churches, and at festivals. He is the founder of the American Story Theater, and teaches a course at the Rhode Island School of Design called "Telling Lies."

Mark lives in Providence, Rhode Island with his wife and three children.

---

You may order additional copies of **A Hanukkah Present**, as well as Mark Binder's other works, including:

**The Brothers Schlemiel • The Bedtime Story Book
Classic Stories for Boys and Girls
Tall Tales, Whoppers and Lies • Dead at Knotty Oak**

*These fine books and audio recordings are available from your local bookstore or favorite online provider, including Amazon.Com, CDBaby.com, Audible.com and the iTunes music store.*

*You may also order directly from
www.lightpublications.com*

CPSIA information can be obtained at www.ICGtesting.com
Printed in the USA
BVOW08*0438191015

422943BV00003B/18/P